I0581325

Sassy Supplies Cozy Mysteries Books 1-4

Katherine Brown

Costumes

&

Cadavers

Katherine H. Brown

Costumes & Cadavers

Copyright © 2022 by Katherine Brown

Book design by Katherine Brown Books

First Printing, 2022

www.katherinebrownbooks.com

One

A peal of wicked laughter echoing down the hall. Three of my guests jumped, looking over their shoulders.

I laughed lightly, glad I'd taken the time to hook up the awesome Halloween doorbell.

"I'll be right back." Excusing myself from the party, I scooped up a big bowl of candy on my way to the front door.

I happily handed out candy to three witches, Buzz Lightyear, the headless horseman, and Thor. Thor seemed to have lost some muscle tone since the last Avengers movie but, hey, who was I to judge. Many of the costume I'd seen on my doorstep were homemade, while others had clearly cost a fortune in cosplay items.

I looked down at my own costume as I shut the door and placed the candy bowl on a side table. I'd chosen to be *Game of Thrones* character Daenerys Targaryen, sewing a passable copy of one of the few blue dresses she wore, complete with a deep v-neckline. The textured material draped to the floor, allowing me to wear pants and tall boots beneath it like she did. What really sold the outfit were the intricate braids I'd taken time to put in my extremely light brown hair. Light, light, light brown. I'm not a blonde; that's my story, and I'm sticking to it.

Homemade Halloween was the party theme; after all, employees and customers of my hobbies and crafts store, Sassy Supplies, had been invited. It only made sense to encourage a little extra craftiness in our costumes, and if that happened to sell more supplies and be a boost for business, so be it.

My musings were interrupted by a scream coming from around the back of the house. I took off running.

"What? What is it?" I asked, racing up to Margo, one of our best customers.

She laughed. "Don't worry. Your skeleton decoration just scared Rita, that's all."

"It wasn't just the skeleton, which by the way, I nearly tripped over," Margo's twin sister Rita said shakily.

Their mother had been a real lush before she died. In the delivery room, when the doctor told her she was having twins, she called for a margarita and passed out. Unfortunately, the girls' father wasn't the brightest bulb, so he put down the names he thought she wanted on the birth certificate—Margo and Rita.

I followed Rita's pointing finger as she kept talking. "That ghost cat nearly gave me a heart attack too, appearing out of nowhere."

Sure enough, my white fluffy Persian really did look ethereal against the dark night, batting at something long and slender near the skeleton decoration. The only problem was, I didn't have any skeleton decorations.

***

"Jinx," I crooned. "Jinx, come here, baby."

Nothing.

My adorably flat-faced feline gave me a look communicating such disdain that I nearly rolled my eyes. Being a cat owner was not great for self-esteem, that's for sure.

"Margo, can you take Rita and the others back in the house, please? Tell everyone to gather in the living room for the costume judging. I'll be there after I grab Jinx."

"Costume contest judging in the living room!" Margo hollered. "Come on! Move it! Let's go!" She turned and winked to me as she ushered the four or five guests back into the house.

Quiet and Margo didn't go together. Even her costume, a loud disco diva outfit that might have made the seventies shudder, couldn't hold a candle to her boisterous personality.

Once everyone was inside, I reached around Jinx and took the long silver object from between his paws, earning myself an irritated mewl.

"Where in the world did you get this X-acto knife?" I asked him. Unable to ignore the bad feeling any longer, I leaned over and lifted the skull mask from the person lying in my backyard, praying that at any moment they would jump up and yell "Gotcha!" for the world's worst Halloween prank.

When Nate Connor's face appeared beneath the mask, I gasped. A customer, and a bit of a jerk, he would be just the type to go in for a bad prank. Unfortunately, he didn't move, and I could tell by the gash in his throat that he wouldn't be moving ever again.

I pushed down the sick feeling of all my Halloween candy wanting to come back up and stepped away from the body. Fishing my cell out of my back pocket, which would be difficult enough to reach beneath my dress without also trying to hold tightly to my wriggling cat, I at last called 911.

A strong floral scent clung to the air, and I vaguely wondered which of my flowers might have been blooming so late in the year. I didn't see any, but then again, it was dark already. I plunked myself down numbly at the patio table, waiting for the police to arrive.

That's where Grampy found me minutes later. "There you are. You've got people waiting on you, including me. Let's go, Chare-bear."

My grandfather had moved in with me six months prior to Halloween, when my grandmother passed away. He was still in pretty good shape for eighty-four, but he didn't like living alone. That night, he volunteered to co-judge the costume contest with me for the Halloween party. It doesn't matter that I'm almost twenty-seven years old or that I own my own business. To Grampy, I'll always be his little bitty granddaughter.

"Actually, I need you to do the judging without me."

What I wanted to tell him was to simply send all of our guests away, but I figured there might be a little truth in TV murder-mysteries showing the police wanting everyone to remain at the scene to give a statement. So, I opted to keep my guests oblivious.

Did that make everyone present a suspect? Once I began to think about it, I did begin to freak out. Was there a murderer at my party?

Grampy noticed, of course. Sharp as a tack, that man. "Charity, you're shaking. What's the matter?"

"Nothing."

"Don't you nothing me, young lady. Something's up; that's as clear as crystal. Now, you can tell me what it is, or I can go in there and clear out the guests by telling them you are having some kind of woman problems and need them to leave." He crossed his arms stubbornly.

Sharp as a tack and stubborn as a mule, I amended my thoughts.

Sighing, I spilled, "The police are on their way, Grampy. There's a dead guy over by the bushes. And I think Jinx has blood on his fur." It was true. As I sat holding my cat, I couldn't help but notice the rust-colored spots matting his paws and parts of his leg. I shuddered.

Grampy wrapped me in a hug. "Don't worry. The police will sort this out. Are you hurt?"

"No, I'm just shaken."

Jinx, obviously tired of having his freedom restricted, mewled loudly again. I handed him to Grampy, pushing them both toward the door.

"Can you put Jinx in the laundry room on your way to the costume judging, please? I'll wait here for the police. It's fine. I promise." Knowing he was about to argue, I put on my most pleading face, the face that never failed to get me an ice cream cone as a kid. "I don't want any of the guests coming back out, please, Grampy?"

Two

Hearing the police cars pull up, I walked to the fence and opened the gate between the back yard and the front. "Back here," I called.

"Mrs. Basham?"

"Miss," I automatically corrected the moustached officer. By his tone and the orders that he barked out to the other men in tow, I gathered he was the officer in charge.

"Miss Basham, then. I'm Officer Johnson. You said there was a Halloween party here tonight?"

I nod. "Still is, technically. I sent everyone inside."

"Okay. Did you find the body?"

"No, one of my guests tripped over it." I remembered Jinx. "Oh, and my cat was near it, too. He was playing with this. The cat was playing, not Nate, the body."

I handed over the X-acto knife, but instead of taking it, Officer Johnson motioned another man to come over. The gentleman held out a clear plastic bag for me to drop it into.

"Please go wait inside with the others, but don't say anything about the dead man." Officer Johnson instructed with barely a glance in my direction as he eyed my backyard. "Officer Sota will be in shortly to begin taking statements."

Dismissed, I entered the kitchen, leaning on the door and taking a deep breath. *Act normal. Act normal. What exactly is normal supposed to feel like after you find someone dead?* My thoughts were spinning. Thankfully, Jinx chose that moment to escape from the laundry room. Apparently, Grampy hadn't shut the door completely. As Jinx rubbed against my legs, I pulled myself together. Time to join the others.

Grampy caught my eye and I gave a brief shake of my head. We didn't need to say anything. He understood immediately and smoothly continued the costume contest. I tried to pay attention, truly, but standing in a room, wondering if you were next to a killer, really did a number on a girl's nerves.

Relief coursed through me when Officer Sota finally let himself in and took over. Jet black hair cut neat, almost military-style, a stare that felt as deep as his voice sounded, tanned skin with a few freckles on his nose and arms, and a poker face that would have me sweating in no time; those were my first impressions of Officer Sota. Surely, with him doing the questioning they would arrest someone, and this nightmare would be over soon.

Two hours later, I realized I couldn't have been more wrong. It took almost fifteen minutes for Officer Sota, and eventually me and Grampy, to convince everyone it wasn't some part of the party, that Nate Connor was, in fact, dead. After that, chaos erupted with screams and gasps and a crush of people trying to get out. Judging by the two additional officers posted at the front door who refused to let anyone leave, panic must be a regular reaction to murder.

I sat at my kitchen table, wondering if it would ever feel pleasant to sit there again, as I answered Officer Sota's questions for the second time. Thorough is one thing, but that felt more like the third degree of suspicion.

Closing his small notepad, the officer looked up at me. "I think that's about it. We will need you to come to the station tomorrow morning and be fingerprinted, so we can eliminate your prints from those found at the scene."

"Oh. Okay." After Officer Sota left, I walked through the empty downstairs, listlessly picking up empty cups and plates, putting away food, and trying to rid myself of all thoughts of death.

Seeing Grampy slumped in a chair by the stairs, fast asleep where he'd sat waiting on me, finally brought a smile back to my face. I draped a throw blanket across him and went up to bed.

Three

Saturday morning, I sat in the parking lot and stared at the police station before going inside. A small, squat, brown brick building, it didn't seem as intimidating as I'd expected it to.

"Hi, I'm here to be fingerprinted." I smiled at the older gentleman sitting behind the desk in the lobby. He didn't smile back.

"Name?"

"Charity Basham."

Flipping over a clipboard, he scanned a list of names. Finding mine quickly at the top, the officer nodded. "Second door on your left."

"Thank you." My shoes echoed on the linoleum floor as I made my way down the hall. I found the second door wide open. "Knock, knock." I called out, entering.

A pretty woman with oriental features and satiny black hair motioned me forward. "Good morning. You must be Charity."

"Yes. I was told to be fingerprinted today?"

The woman smiled. "You're in the right spot."

She rattled off some information about the process and asked me to fill out and sign a quick form, saying that I understood.

"Now that we have that out of the way, the rest is a piece of cake." I stood awkwardly as she took my hand and, one at a time, rolled the pads of my fingers over a machine that scanned them.

Snatches of conversation floated in from the hallway. My ears perked up when I heard the name of my store. I strained to hear more.

"You say the murder weapon definitely came from Sassy Supplies?"

"Yes, sir."

"Okay. We'll need to interview all of the employees again. And the owner."

"Miss?" A little tug on my hand clued me in that I'd been paying too much attention to the outside. "Miss. I said we're all through here."

"Great!" I hurried to the door, calling thanks over my shoulder. Looking both ways, I spotted Officer Sota turning a corner. He must have been one of the people I overheard. I rushed after him.

He was disappearing through another door when I caught sight of him again. I sprinted faster, just making it inside as the door closed automatically.

"Hey!" A woman at a desk in front of me shouted and stood up.

Suddenly, I was looking at the wrong end of her pistol.

I threw my hands in the hair. "Wait! Don't shoot me, please. I just wanted to talk to Officer Sota."

"You can't be in here." The woman glared.

My surroundings slowly came into focus. The linoleum flooring was gone. The wall hangings were gone. Instead, bare concrete floors and cinderblock walls interspersed with barred cells met my gaze. I'd walked straight back into the jail. With the criminals. Yikes!

"Lower your weapon, Corporal," Officer Sota told the woman as he strode back toward the commotion – a.k.a. me.

"I'm sorry." I looked between the two. "I was trying to catch Officer Sota." Turning to him, I held my arms out in a helpless gesture. "I heard you say the murder weapon was from my store. I can't believe it."

Officer Sota took me by the elbow. "Roll door," he barked, and the door we came through opened again. He let me go and gestured that I follow him to an office. "Have a seat."

It sounded more like a command than an offer.

I sat, irritated, and jumped right to the point. "I thought I heard you saying Nate's murder weapon came from my store? That can't be true. How could you even know that?. It's an X-acto knife—pretty standard craft supply. I bet even Wal-Mart carries them." I crossed my arms with satisfaction.

"Do you always eavesdrop? Or barge into off-limits areas?"

"No." I shifted uncomfortably. "But I couldn't help it. Seriously, why are you assuming it came from my store?"

"What makes you think I'm assuming anything?"

I glared. "Don't you know it's rude to answer a question with a question?"

"Is it?"

That guy was really getting under my skin. "Yes," I bit out. "It is."

Officer Sota shrugged. "Well, let me ask you another one. Why do you think the knife is standard?"

"Isn't it?" I quipped. Two could play that game.

"The handle maybe. The blade is a specialty one, not sold as part of the standard set. Only one store in town carries these in particular."

Gulp. Maybe my righteous indignation had been premature.

"Oh."

Officer Sota leaned forward. "While I've got you here, Miss Basham, do you have any witnesses as to your whereabouts during the party between 8:30 and 9:15 last night?"

"Me? I was back and forth between rooms and answering the door for trick-or-treaters. I'm sure people must have seen me."

Making some notes, he asked, "Did anyone help you pass out candy?"

"No."

The sight of a pen swirling over a notepad had never looked so ominous as he scribbled.

"Do I need a lawyer?" I added.

"Do you?"

Exasperated, I tossed my hands up. "I didn't kill Nate, if that's what you want to know. Why are you acting like I'm a suspect? Oh my gosh! Am I a suspect? This can't be right."

"Let me be blunt, since you seem to continue questioning whether or not I can do my job." Officer Sota counted on his fingers, each statement sounding like a bang of a gavel or the clank of a jail cell as he painted a pretty clear picture for me. "Your hair was found on the body, your prints are the only ones on the murder weapon, the murder weapon came from a store that you happen to own, and the murder occurred at your residence. Plus, your cat's fur is on the body as well."

Shakily, I said, "When you put it like that, maybe I do need a lawyer."

"Maybe you do." He nodded to the door. "For now, you're free to go. Don't leave town."

Four

"Morning, Charity!"

Gwen, my best clerk, arrived to work in a cloud of perfume, as usual. I coughed. "New scent?" I asked.

"Yes!" she squealed, sniffing her own wrist. "Don't you love it? It's called Lasting Ambition. I needed something different."

"It is lasting; that's for sure." Over the years, I'd given up trying to hint that just a drop was more than enough. Gwen and hints were like oil and water.

"Your hair looked amazing last night, by the way," Gwen said, stuffing her purse into a locker in the breakroom. Purple and black, the purse matched her strapless romper to perfection. I couldn't wear strapless anything; it would fall right off of me.

"Thanks. I'll admit, it took a lot longer to do those braids than I thought it would. I didn't see you at the party though. Did I miss you?"

Gwen shook her head. "No, I couldn't make it. Saw pictures though. Never would have taken you for the Daenerys type, so bloodthirsty."

At the word blood, I shivered involuntarily. "Me? Definitely not. I liked her earlier character much better than the ending one. I'm just a sucker for sewing interesting clothes. Anyway," I changed the subject. "Can you cover the floor today? Becca is going to be late."

Becca, the only other clerk, had called to say the police wanted her in for an interview. She was on the verge of hysterics, and if she made it in at all, I would have been shocked. Still, it wasn't like our business was often booming.

Gwen clearly had the same thought. "No problem. I can handle our regulars and we don't have any sales going on that would bring in major crowds."

"Great. Thanks."

We worked quietly, stocking new merchandise. When it was time to open, I unlocked the door. "

I'll be in the office if you need me," I told Gwen.

She waved from behind the register, popping a stick of gum in her mouth. The bell over the entrance jingled as I slipped into the office, closing the door behind me.

I sat down at the computer and waited for it to fire up. The thing was a dinosaur, and I made another mental note to look into costs of laptops or tablets. Signing in, I went through my usual routine of checking emails, answering questions, and printing out new orders. Before I could begin to sort through them, my cell rang.

Grampy's deep voice jumped through the line before I could even say hello. "Chare-Bear, are you busy?"

I smiled. "Hey, Grampy. I'm never too busy for you. What's up?"

"You remember Jerry from my poker group, right?"

"Of course. How is Jerry?"

"He's fine, fine." Grampy's voice lowered to a whisper. "Jerry still works for the police, in evidence. Chare-Bear, I think you may have a problem. Jerry called me this morning and said those cops are saying the murder weapon came from Sassy Supplies."

Touched that Grampy was worried about me, I told him about my conversation with Officer Sota earlier. "So, thanks for calling, but I don't know what else I can do about it. I wish I knew what was so special about the blade that they were able to track it to my store, though."

"Jerry told me that, too."

"Really? Why didn't you say so? I'm all ears, Grampy." As he rattled off a number for the blade, I grabbed a pen and made notes. "A #26 blade used for whittling, you said? Uh-huh. Okay. Great. Yep, I'll call you later."

Excitement tingled through me. I could sort through our records and find out who had bought this blade. I'd be able to clear my name in no time!

Pop.

"Aighh!!" I whirled around in my chair, hands flailing karate style. Or what I pictured to be karate style, since I'd never taken a lesson.

"Whoa," Gwen backed up. "Sorry, I didn't mean to scare you. I knocked, but you didn't answer."

She blew another bubble and I scowled, thinking we might need a rule about no gum-chewing during work. "What can I do for you, Gwen?"

"I'm going to get lunch at the taco truck down the street. Do you want anything?" she offered.

"No, thanks." I shook my head.

"Okay. You should probably come watch the register while I'm gone. People have been pouring in."

Surprised, I asked, "Really?"

"Yeah. Seems Nate dying at your party is big news."

I grimaced.

Peering over my shoulder, Gwen pointed to my hasty notes. "What are you working on?"

"Oh, nothing really. Grampy just called and told me what blade was used to kill Nate since it came from our store."

"You don't say? Well," another bubble, "I'm off for food. Text me if you need me."

"Enjoy your lunch, Gwen," I told her, stuffing the paper into my pocket.

Not two seconds after she walked out, I winced. I shouldn't have told her about the knife blade. Hopefully, Officer Sota wouldn't find out. Could you be arrested for talking?

The lunch rush was even busier than Gwen predicted. A few people came in simply to gossip and made no bones about it, but most liked to at least give the appearance of shopping before trying to weasel bits of information out of me. So,

Sassy Supplies was having a record sales day. It spoke sad volumes about humanity when murder is better for business than advertising.

I sighed as the last two customers left with their heat transfer vinyl and canvas tote bags. I tried not to divulge too much information. Officer Sota's face as he told me not to discuss the case kept popping into my mind, and I didn't want to be on the receiving end of a lecture from him.

Glancing at my watch, I was shocked to see it was an hour past Gwen's lunch break. I checked my phone. Sure enough, a short, staccato text from her waited.

Called to police station for questions. Not sure when be done. Can I take the day?

I typed out a reply that I'd see her back in the store the next day and slipped my phone back into my pocket. Realizing the police had probably called Erica, my other clerk, for questions, too, I decided to just manage the store myself and not worry about calling her in on her day off.

No sooner had I sat down to rest my aching feet than the bell jingled again.

In walked Margo and Rita. Margo was dolled up as usual, her red hair curled and framing her face, complimenting the black jumper she wore with red heels. Rita's style was usually extremely relaxed in comparison, but she looked downright frumpy in an oversized sweater a horrible Halloween orange shade that did nothing for her light complexion. Her hair, a shade lighter than Margo's, looked like she'd barely run a brush through it, and I could tell that the socks peeking out over her sneakers didn't match at all.

"Hello, ladies." I greeted them.

"Don't get up for us, Charity." Margo waved me back onto my stool as I rose. "We can shop in a bit. First, we came in to see how you're holding up. My cousin Ace said that you got questioned by the cops today."

Rita didn't say anything. She looked tense but nodded sympathetically. Quieter than Margo, obviously, Rita was also sweetness itself on most days.

However, that day there was no friendly smile, no kind compliment. Something about her seemed off.

I frowned. "I wouldn't say I was questioned, per say. My trip to the police station was standard to give my fingerprints. Actually, I had a few questions for the detective while I was there." I refused to let my customers believe I was an actual suspect, even if I thought I might be. "I don't think I know your cousin?" Letting the question linger, I waited for Margo to fill in the blanks.

She did, of course. "Ace is a bit of a gambler. And a cheat. He was sitting in holding this morning. They brought him in to dry out a bit after breaking up a fight he was in last night. Anyway, they let him go around lunch, and he swung by the Cut and Chat on his way home. Told me that a hot blonde with hair so long it'd probably never seen a pair of scissors stormed right into the jail this morning, yelling about a murder, and then got hauled away for questioning." Margo shrugged. "I knew it was you right away. Don't worry, I set him straight. Told him I trim your hair regularly every six weeks, and that it is healthy, happy hair."

"First, I am not blonde," I began. "My hair is light, light, light, light brown, as you know. Second, I wasn't yelling, exactly. Simply, voicing my shock. Loudly."

Rita sniffled. "We were all shocked about Nate."

Not bothering to correct her about what specifically had shocked me, I leaned past the counter and patted her shoulder. "I'm very sorry for your loss," I told her.

"Excuse me." She gave another sniffle and walked quickly back out the door.

"I best go after her," Margo rolled her eyes. "Oh, there should be an online order ready under Rita's name. Can you check please?"

"Sure, what was it? Do you know?" We kept things organized in tubs by department. Knowing what I was looking for would make finding the order quicker. Organizing by name might have made more sense, but we didn't have that many tubs or space for them.

"I believe it was a chunk of wood and some whittling supplies."

"Whittling?" I nearly yelped.

Margo looked at me as if I'd gone bananas. "You have something against whittling?"

"No. Of course not." I couldn't tell her about the case. *What to say, what to say?* "When did she start whittling? I'm impressed, that's all."

"I'm not sure that she did. I think it was for Nate." Margo shrugged. "Oh! Maybe I should leave it here, in case it reminds her of him again. She hasn't been herself since that night at your party." Margo wrung her hands together.

Seeing her flustered made me uneasy. Margo was never flustered. Blustery, yes. Sputtering, spluttering, even occasionally thundering, sure. Flustered never. Was her quiet sister really so upset that Margo would worry? Or was something else bothering Rita so much that it put Margo out of sorts?

Five

Closing time finally came. I grabbed my purse and phone, locked the front door, and dragged my tired self to my car on dead feet. Exhausted, not to mention hungry since I had never eaten lunch, I had printed out the last six months' worth of orders to go through at home.

Delicious aromas wafted to me as I walked into the house. "Grampy!" I shouted. "I'm home."

Jinx strolled casually into the hall, waiting for me to greet him since rushing to welcome me home would have been much too undignified a show of affection for my pompous pussy cat.

"And hello to you, Jinx." Rubbing from his head to his tail, I lavished a few overdue attentions, receiving a low grumbling purr of satisfaction, before I obeyed the much louder grumbling of my stomach and hightailed it to the kitchen.

Grampy was busy at the counter, his back to me.

"Is that a Pizza Palace box I see?" I licked my lips. Pizza. A girl's best friend.

Grampy waggled his eyebrows. "No. It's two." He spun around, cackling like a spry chicken, holding another Pizza Palace box and plates. "One is supper. Would you like to guess what the other is?"

"You didn't?" Not daring to say it out loud, I reached for the box on the table, tugging the lid open. "You did!" I squealed, unashamedly excited. "Chocolate chip dessert pizza. You're the best."

"Obviously," Grampy rolled his eyes. "Come on, before it gets cold."

After consuming more than my fair share of pizza, I filled Grampy in on the day, the excess customers, and the surprising fact that quiet, unassuming Rita was one of the customers who ordered whittling supplies.

"Who were the others?" he asked, reaching for his second slice of chocolate chip pizza.

"I don't know yet, actually. Being tied up at the register all day, I never got the chance to go through our orders." I licked my chocolate-covered fingers before pulling the papers out of my purse. "I brought a lot home to look through as a start though."

"Want me to help, Chare-Bear?" Grampy asked as I started flipping through them.

"No, no, no." Groaning, I slumped my head onto the table.

"Well, sorry for offering."

Sitting back up, I shook my head. "Not you. I just realized that I sorted the list in alphabetical order by department before printing them."

Grampy's brow furrowed. "What's so bad about that?"

"Nothing. Except the papers stop at the letter S for sewing." I tossed the papers in the trash. "For some reason, the rest of the list didn't print."

"It'll hold 'til tomorrow, kiddo."

"No. I need to go back to the store and print the rest of the list." *Might as well have that fourth piece of dessert pizza.* It was turning into one of those days. After swallowing a few bites, I explained. "The faster we have new suspects, the faster Officer Sota can take my name off of his list."

"You go on." Grampy said. "I'll clean up. But take Jinx with you. Danged cat's been curled up in my chair all day, acting like he owns the place. Probably there now. You know he doesn't like it when I move him."

"Okay." I wrapped my arms around Grampy for a quick hug. "Back in a flash."

Sure enough, I found Jinx in the living room, lounging in the recliner as accused.

"You and I are going on an outing," I told him.

Slowly raising his head, Jinx stared at me and then blinked slowly. I took that as agreement and scooped him into a pet taxi.

Six

Sassy Supplies, as well as both stores on either side of it, was all darkness behind the front windows, as it should have been. Still, the blackness unnerved me as I unlocked the door and entered the store, not wanting to turn on the light lest people think we were open. I hadn't gone in the back door, because it had a tendency to stick and I didn't want to deal with it that late at night.

I sat the pet taxi down and opened the door for Jinx, taking an extra moment to turn on my cell's flashlight. Before I had time to stand back up, Jinx's tail waved agitatedly back and forth, back and forth.

"Hey!" I hissed as my cat companion abandoned me and took off at a run—well a lope, which for a laid-back animal like Jinx might as well be a run—and deserted me there in the front of the store. "There better not be a mouse in my store," I grumbled as I followed after my fickle feline.

I entered the employee's only door and registered a dim light spilling out of the back-office seconds before a shriek from the same location made me jump.

"Get away, you creepy cat!"

Hearing the yell, I promptly raced to the office to save Jinx, only to stop short with surprise.

"Gwen?" I felt my eyebrows shoot up at seeing my clerk slapping the air between her and Jinx with a sheaf of papers.

Startled, she looked up at me and dropped the papers, which fluttered haphazardly around the room.

My racing heart slowed as I heaved a sigh of relief. "Girl, you nearly gave me a heart attack. What are you doing here so late?"

Gwen's eyes flitted around the room, landing on her cell phone beneath the lamp on my desk. "Forgot my phone," she said, snatching it up and slipping it into her pocket.

"Oh. Hey, wait a minute," I narrowed my eyes. "Didn't you text me from your phone today? *After* you already left Sassy Supplies?"

Gwen shrugged nonchalantly, and her attitude made me question my own memory. I looked down at my phone, still in my hand with the flashlight turned on. Maybe I needed to recheck the message dates.

I froze.

The flashlight was pointed at one of the many papers Gwen had dropped, papers that happened to be the rest of the purchase orders and inventory lists I'd neglected to grab from my desk that afternoon. And there, staring up at me in bold black letters, was the section concerning whittling. Only four names. One leapt out at me like the boogie man himself.

Gwen Sherman.

I looked up, taking an involuntary step backward.

"You really shouldn't have come back to work tonight," Gwen grumbled. "It ruins everything."

Before I knew what was happening, Gwen lunged at me, wrapping her purple-painted fingers around my throat. From this close, I also noticed she had a new nose piercing.

Her perfume was so overwhelming up close that I might have died, unable to breathe without the extra help from her hands. Gasping for air either way, I tried to shake her off. Suddenly, she let out a screech and let go on her own. I looked down to see Jinx, silently sharpening his nails on her bare legs. I could have kissed that ball of fur.

Gwen wasn't feeling so loving. She kicked Jinx. Hard. As my cat careened across the room, I let out a howl of anger and knocked Gwen upside the head with the only thing I had, my phone. It was hard enough to leave a mark but otherwise only served to make her madder.

I didn't see the slap coming. My head snapped to the side, and pain bloomed along my cheek. I felt warmth dripping and touched a finger to my face to find blood. The plethora of rings Gwen wore were no doubt to thank for that gash. I backed up.

Why, oh why didn't I use my phone to call 911 instead of hitting her? I berated myself. Of course, I knew the answer to that. She hurt my cat. Instinct had taken over. Even then, Jinx's slumped form wrenched my heart. I couldn't help him if I didn't find a way to stop Gwen, though. Channelling every Jackie Chan movie that I'd ever watched, I swung my leg out between her ankles.

My foot connected; unfortunately, it wasn't enough to sweep her legs out from under her. "Ow!" We both yelled at the same time.

Movies lied.

I had a feeling a new bruise was forming on my shin. I resolved right then to sign up for actual karate lessons. If I survived the night, that was.

Out of ideas, I decided to try talking to her instead. Maybe I could convince her she didn't have to hurt me, or kill me, or whatever her crazy intentions were.

"Gwen," I eased my hands up in front of me, trying to calm her. "Let's hold on a minute. You don't want to hurt me. You probably didn't want to hurt Nate either. I'm sure we can work this out."

"You're wrong," she snapped. "I *didn't* want to hurt you, but now you know too much. Plus, you have to pay for beaming me in the head. And I did want to hurt Nate. I'm only disappointed it had to be quick, and he didn't have to go through the pain he deserved, the pain that he put me through."

"I don't understand." I pushed back strands of sweaty hair that had fallen from my ponytail as I shook my head. "What did Nate do to you?"

"He betrayed me!" Gwen yelled.

Confused, I asked, "Betrayed you how?"

"He started dating that mousy, fashion-challenged Rita. And he didn't tell me. He said he loved me. Then the next week, in that hussy comes buying whittling tools. Nate is our only customer who whittles, besides some online buyer in another town." Gwen shook, fury radiating from her. "His birthday was coming up. She bought him the exact gift that I did. And as if that wasn't bad enough, I confronted him at your party. I brought his birthday gift. I even told him that I loved him. You know what he did? He told me that I could keep the gift." Gwen's voice rose, a high-pitched fevered sound, as she spoke faster. "Then, he told me that he wasn't going to see me on his birthday; he planned to cancel on me and spend his birthday with her. Told me at least now he wouldn't need to remember to call and cancel because I already knew."

"I'm so sorry," I said, unsure what else to say. As she talked, I inched closer to Jinx, little by little.

"Not as sorry as Nate. He'll never get to hurt anyone again." Gwen smiled. Actually smiled. "Don't you see? I had to kill him. I had to put a stop to the lies spewing up his throat and out his mouth. So, I cut them off. One slice. Done. No more lies, no more betrayal."

"Mmm," I murmured. I darted my eyes to my cat again. Relief seeped into my heart as I detected a small rise and fall of his chest.

"Are you even listening to me?" Gwen screeched.

Eyes snapping back to hers, I nodded quickly. "Of course. Nate was a jerk. He was a liar. You didn't deserve that. Nobody does." I rambled all of the agreeable things I could think of, all the while hoping she would just keep talking until I figured out a plan. Quick under pressure, clearly I was not.

She relaxed a little. "Exactly. So, you understand, right? I had no choice." To my horror, her face hardened again. "Just like I have no choice now."

As she menaced toward me, her foot came down on Jinx's tail, and it revived him like nothing else could have. Leaping into the air, Jinx launched himself at Gwen again. That time, she stumbled and fell.

Snatching Jinx up, I ran as fast as I could for the back door, praying it was unlocked and unstuck from when Gwen came in. It was. I slammed through it and smacked right into a hot brick wall. Well, not exactly. My hands pressed against a muscled chest, and my eyes met Officer Sota's, only an inch above my own.

"She's trying to kill me," I blurted.

The heat from his chest was replaced by a chill November wind as he moved me to the side of the door and drew his weapon. I heard Gwen's racing footsteps before I saw her.

"Stop, police. Come out with your hands up," Officer Sota commanded loudly, not quite a yell but reverberating with authority.

Gwen was evidently too close to the door or didn't care, because her footsteps never let up. Just as she rushed outside, I stuck my foot out. Down she went.

Officer Sota sent me a puzzled look, even as he bent down to handcuff Gwen.

To his unspoken question, I merely shrugged. "She kicked my cat."

Officer Sota stared at me for two seconds, and then a wide grin split his face. Shaking his head, lips twitching with mirth that I'd never expected to see in the serious officer, he read Gwen her rights and hauled her to an unmarked car.

"Will you be okay?" he asked.

A man had been murdered. At my house. And for a time, I was a suspect. Then, the real murderer, a woman who I employed and considered a friend, tried to kill me. In my own store. I didn't know if I would ever be okay. But then, I knew that wasn't what he was asking.

I smiled. "I'll be fine. My car is around front."

He gave a brief nod.

"Hey!" I called.

"Yes?"

"How did you know to be here?" I asked him.

He pointed at Gwen's Volkswagen Beetle. "BOLO out on the car. Her alibi didn't check out, and one of the guests saw her briefly at your party, though Miss Sherman specifically said she hadn't been there."

"Okay. Thanks." I waved as he drove away. Going inside, I locked up the back door and turned the light off in my office. It was in shambles, but I felt pretty close to shambles myself. Cleaning could wait until the next day.

Jinx stuck right to my ankles all the way until I loaded him in the pet taxi up front. I made a mental note to pick up some shrimp and lobster kitty delicacies.

As I cranked the car, my phone rang. Grampy.

"Hey Chare-Bear, where are you?" he asked. "I have to say, I'm about to eat the last piece of dessert pizza if you don't get back soon."

I sighed. "I'm on my way, Grampy. I'm on my way. And trust me, I need that chocolate chip pizza way more than you do. You aren't going to believe what I have to tell you."

The End

Turkeys
&
Tragedy

Katherine H. Brown

Turkeys & Tragedy

Editing by Richelle Braswell Comprehensive Editing, www.RichelleBraswell.com
Cover image by Canva images.
Book design by Katherine Brown Books

First Printing, 2021

www.katherinebrownbooks.com

One

"Pass me the orange bandana, please." Bunny tapped her granddaughter, Kira, on the shoulder, asking again. "Can you please pass me the orange one?"

"Hmm? Oh, sure. Here." Kira handed over the material and continued sulking.

I beamed at the turnout for this month's craft night at my little store, Sassy Supplies. It had been a fantastic idea to invite internet DIY decorating celebrity Serena Jackson to the store to teach a craft on making turkey wreaths the Saturday before Thanksgiving. I made a mental note to find Becca and thank her for the suggestion. Becca, my only remaining clerk since I hadn't gotten around to hiring another yet, had really been going above and beyond lately, working extra hours and helping deliver local orders. Barely out of high school, she was waiting until she had more money saved up to start college next year. When I'd voiced my idea about having someone new come in to host a craft this month, she had immediately recommended Serena.

Speaking of Serena, she approached me now. Her silky brown hair fell in curls halfway down her back and her heels, maroon to match the pantsuit she wore, click-clicked across the linoleum floor.

"Hey," I greeted her. "It looks like the wreaths are a real winner."

"They're too cute not to love and too simple not to attract a crowd." She shrugged one shoulder like they were no big deal. Flicking a strand of hair out of her face, she surveyed the room. "Do you think you could help out over at table four? That lady can't seem to make a single decision by herself. Jenny is swamped helping table two and I need to run to your ladies' room."

I looked over to table four, which happened to have two of my regulars and a new girl I hadn't met yet working on wreaths, and agreed. "The restroom is in the back right corner," I told her.

Serena hadn't been what I expected. When I thought of crafts, well, I thought of casual, relaxed, regular people. Like Serena's young assistant, Jenny Michaels. The petite woman was dressed in jeans and an oversized tan sweater, the effect made her look small, soft, and approachable. Serena, on the other hand, was all business, dressed to the nines and running the class on a pretty quick timetable. I'd thought maybe that was just her YouTube persona, but we weren't filming.

On the way to table four, I passed Jenny helping Bunny Neugenbauer with the knots for her bandana wreath. Bunny was a sweet grandmotherly woman with wire-rimmed, rose gold glasses forever perched in her curly silver hair that was cut close to her head. She never missed a craft night. I noticed Bunny had managed to drag her seventeen-year-old granddaughter, Kira, in with her this month. The girl sat with her phone in her lap beneath the table, texting, her wreath basically untouched, a deep frown on her purple lips. Another new face sat on the other side of Bunny. Similar in age to Bunny, she wore her gray hair in a medium bob and had a crocheted pink and yellow shawl on. It looked handmaid to my trained eye. From the way they were chatting, I assumed she and Bunny were friends prior to tonight.

"Hey, Dana! Bill, nice of you to join us tonight." I stood before my two regulars at table four.

"Not like I had much choice. Danged woman threatened to cancel Thanksgiving dinner if she didn't have this turkey wreath." Bill obligingly cut the length of ribbon his wife held out for him, shaking his head. "Blackmail, that's what it is."

Technically, Bill wasn't really a regular crafter or customer, just regularly annoyed his wife was dragging him to Sassy Supplies again. A year or so ago, Dana had been in a wreck and now was afraid to drive. Though he grumbled about it, Bill drove her wherever she wanted to go. They were in their seventies, and as far as I could tell, he took good care of his wife. I thought it was very sweet.

"Charity, I need your opinion," Dana said. "Do you think this is too much orange ribbon and not enough red?"

"I think it is perfect," I gestured to a fat roll of ribbon on the table. "If you're worried, you could add a bit more of this brown between them, so each color stands out better."

"Good idea." Dana nodded. "Here, cut five of these lengths will you, hon?"

Bill sighed dramatically, making me stifle a chuckle, but he measured and cut just as his wife asked.

I switched my focus to the newcomer sitting at the other end of the table. "Hello. I'm Charity. "I haven't seen you in here before."

The red-haired woman, and I do mean Little Mermaid bright, cartoon-red hair, appeared to be in her late twenties. She smiled widely. "I'm Lola. Nice to meet you. I haven't been here before. Actually, this is my first week in town."

"Welcome! What brings you to Becksville, Texas?"

Lola shrugged. "I needed a change. This is where my car ran out of gas," she said, as if that explained everything.

"I see," I murmured politely.

"Well, let me know if you need any help."

"Thanks."

"Charity. Charity, hon," Dana called loudly. "Do you think I should leave more space for the turkey to fit?" She waved her hand from the other end of the table.

Her question was loud enough most customers must have heard her. Across the room, Becca glanced up from where she was assisting twin sisters. We shared a knowing look.

I hated to admit Serena had a point, but Dana really did struggle to trust her own instincts, bless her heart. She never made a purchase without asking what I thought about it, either.

By the time I'd walked Dana through the rest of her wreath, Bill had visited the restroom and come back, bald head dipping low as he dozed off in his chair. Lola had gotten up to explore the store, returning to ask me about some of our paint supplies that interested her. Looking around, I noticed a majority of the crafters were finishing up, but I didn't see Serena anywhere. Or her assistant, Jenny, for that matter.

I made the rounds quickly, oohing and aahing over all the wreaths; they really were as cute as could be. I'll check the restroom as everyone cleans up their areas. I had barely made it to the first table when a scream cut through the low hum of chatting.

Jenny burst out of the doors that led to the restrooms and storage closet. "She's dead! She's dead!"

Bunny clutched her heart. "My Kira?" she cried, looking between Jenny and the empty chair where her granddaughter had been sitting recently.

"I'm here, Bunny. I'm here." Kira appeared behind Jenny. She crossed her bangle-covered arms over her black Wednesday Addams T-shirt "What's with all the screaming?" The same bored look on her face from earlier made me wonder if the girl had any other expression.

Jenny stumbled haltingly across the room to me, clutching at my shoulders. "Serena's dead!" Her lips trembled.

Two

I passed Jenny over to Becca while I called 911. Because Jenny was basically incoherent other than repeating she's dead over and over, I also decided to see about Serena myself. I suppose I hoped Jenny was wrong. Maybe Serena had fainted and hit her head or, I don't know, something that would make more sense than being dead. In my craft store.

I pushed open the restroom door, but there was no Serena, no body, nothing. Stepping back into the hall, I noticed the storage room door was slightly ajar. As I stepped closer, a sinking feeling settled in the pit of my stomach.

The fluorescent light in the storage room let out a low hum, light flickering between bright and dim. I'd been meaning to fix it. Tiptoeing farther into the room, I called softly, "Serena? Hello?"

Silence.

Any hope of Jenny hallucinating was obliterated as I rounded the end of a shelf and nearly tripped on a slim ankle and fashionable shoe. The ankle, of course, was attached to a leg, the leg to a body, and the body belonged to Serena. I covered my mouth as I stared down at her. Her eyes, open and fixed, were red. As were her lips and several blotches across her face, and down her neck, all the way to the orange bandana tied around her neck. Unless the red splotches came from an allergic reaction, someone had strangled her, I realized shakily. She didn't have a stroke, or a heart attack, or just plain old die. Someone took her life.

DIY star and YouTube sensation Serena Jackson had been murdered in my store while I obliviously talked about ribbon and tulle in the other room. White, dizzy spots circled around my head, and the sinking feeling in my stomach turned to a sick one. Rushing to the bathroom, I splashed cold water on my face, gripping the sink until my breathing calmed and my head stopped swimming. Swallowing down the bile in my throat was more difficult, but I did it.

Doing my best to compose myself, I dried my face, patted my long light, light, light, light brown hair—people thought it was blonde but they were wrong—back into place, and returned to the main part of the store, just in time to see the police arrive through the front door. Detective Sota looked up and saw me; his lips pulled into a tight frown. My stomach clenched again.

The first time I'd met the clean-cut, lean, and serious Detective Sota, he had questioned me about the murder at my Halloween party last month. I'd really been hoping not to repeat that particular dance. As he strode purposefully toward me, leaving the other detective to speak with the customers, I knew my luck wasn't that good. His deep brown eyes threatened to swallow me, confirming my assumption that this was going to be all-business. Fleetingly, I considered how nice it might be to meet the detective anywhere but next to a dead body. *Oh well.*

"Hi," I said resignedly. "Serena is this way. I didn't touch the body or anything. I also didn't kill her, just so we're clear."

Detective Sota waited until we were alone in the back hallway, the doors closing behind us, before speaking. "Why is it, Miss Basham, that I'm here to investigate another unexpected death and I find you?"

"Maybe because it's a small town and you're now the main detective?" I shrugged. Officer Sota when I'd met him, he'd been promoted to detective during the Halloween case.

Deadpan stare in place, he shook his head. "You being at two crime scenes in as many months was the anomaly in that particular question, as you well know."

My usual snark disappeared; it was best not to answer. Besides, it wasn't like I wasn't thinking the same thing. Why does this keep happening? I was beginning to attract bodies like some women attracted men, and I didn't like the feeling one bit.

I hung back by the door when we entered the storage room. No need for me to see Serena sprawled out on my floor again; I'd be seeing it plenty in my nightmares. "Over there." I pointed to the shelf that hid her from view.

Detective Sota disappeared behind it. Seconds ticked away. Then a minute. Then two. At last, he reappeared. "Did you notice anything odd or out of place? Here or in the rest of this back area?"

A quick scan of the storage room and nothing jumped out at me. I knew from checking the bathroom earlier that everything was fine there. "No. Nothing."

"Okay. Let's go back out front." He cordoned off the doors to the back hallway with crime scene tape as we exited.

Instead of immediately rejoining Becca and the crafters, I paused. "She was strangled, wasn't she?"

Detective Sota peered at me closely. "What makes you say that?"

"The bandana." I gulped. "The one, um, around her neck. She wasn't wearing it when she arrived. It doesn't even match her outfit, and she seemed all about matching. Even her shoes matched." I swallowed, hoping to slow my rambling. I was likely still in shock which didn't make it any easier to calm down. "The bandana was one of many that we were using in the craft tonight. People could choose from tulle, ribbons, or bandanas to make their turkey wreaths their own unique style."

"I see." Detective Sota nodded, leading me back toward the group. "You know you can't open for business tomorrow, most likely," he said quietly before we reached hearing distance of anyone.

"Yeah." I frowned. Not that I was in a hurry to get back into a place where murder had been committed. Still, neither did I look forward to sitting at home with nothing to do but think about someone being killed only a room away.

Before I knew what was happening, he deposited me next to Becca and joined his partner in taking statements. Detective Wyn took mine. I tried not to examine the fact that I felt strangely deflated to be talking to the solemn woman instead of continuing my conversation with the handsome Detective Sota. He's already a familiar face. That's all.

After giving their statements and contact information, everyone was released to go home. I pulled Becca aside and let her know we wouldn't be opening tomorrow.

"Charity, I feel so terrible!" With bright pink lipstick and glitter eye shadow, she looked even younger than she was and distraught. "If I hadn't told you to invite Serena here, none of this would be happening."

"We don't know that." I patted the girl on the shoulder. "We don't know anything about why Serena was killed or if it was personal or random."

"Oh my gosh! You think it could be someone just killing random people? Like they might kill more?" Her eyes darted toward the front door then the back as if she expected a serial killer to pop up and start laughing maniacally.

I covered a sigh. "What I think is we need to go home and rest. The police will arrest whoever did this, and we will be back to work in no time. Do you want me to call someone to drive you home?"

"No. Thanks." Still looking shaken, Becca hurried to her car, leaving me to lock up.

The coroner had come and left with the body. Crime scene tape still hung garishly across the back wall and hall doors. And piles of craft supplies were still strewn across the tables since I wasn't allowed to clean anything up. Standing on the sidewalk, I shivered as I glanced at the stack of bandanas through the plateglass windows.

"Can I have those keys?" Detective Sota joined me on the sidewalk, holding out a hand. His partner was already in the car, making notes in a flip book it looked like. Though with the dim parking lot lights, it was difficult to be sure.

"Of course," I said. Separating the keys to the store from the ring, I dropped them in his open palm. "Do I have to come to the station tomorrow or anything?"

He shook his head. "I don't think finishing up with the store will take long. In fact, we should be done by midday. So how about you meet me for lunch tomorrow at Pizza Palace?"

"Lunch?"

"To get your keys back. At one."

"One," I echoed like a particularly dull parrot.

He smirked. "See you then."

Three

"Chare-bear!" Grampy hollered from the living room the moment I arrived home. My grandfather had moved in with me earlier in the year after my grandmother passed away. Said he couldn't abide wandering around their house all alone; made it feel like he was dead too. I would have welcomed him no matter what, but the fact that he was an excellent cook and offered to help pay rent just sweetened the deal.

"Hi, Grampy." I leaned over his recliner to give him a hug. "What's up?"

In the second recliner, Jinx opened one eye and gave me a long look then settled back to sleep. I rubbed his head and received only an angry swat from his paw in return. Someone was grumpier than usual today.

"Did you have a robbery?" Grampy asked, regaining my attention.

"No. Why?" I rubbed my neck, tension from the night already creeping in.

"Jerry called. You remember Jerry, from my poker game, right?"

I had a bad feeling I knew where this was going. "The same Jerry who logs evidence at the police department?"

"That's the one." Grampy closed his recliner and stood up. "Well, Jerry called and said that he was given some evidence to log tonight. A bandana. He told me the label indicated it was from your store."

"Do we have any chocolate?" I asked. "You're not going to believe what I have to tell you, and I could really use some chocolate before I do the telling. A lot of chocolate."

"That bad, huh?"

I sighed. "Worse."

Grampy and I settled into the kitchen with a box of cosmic brownies after I fished some kitty treats out of the cabinet and bribed my cantankerous cat to give me a little more affection. The fluffy

Persian cat flicked his white tail around my ankles, tantamount to a hug for his prickly personality. Cosmic brownies, the ones with the galaxy-colored chocolate chips, were my favorite as a kid, and Grampy still bought them sometimes. After half a brownie, and one reluctant purr from Jinx, I felt like I could start talking about the incident.

"Tonight was the big craft night with the turkey wreaths and the star home decorator, Serena Jackson," I said to jog his memory.

"Okay." He waited patiently for me to continue.

Swallowing another bite of brownie around the lump in my throat, I rambled my way through the rest of the story, telling him how I'd been helping customers and Serena had gone to the restroom and never came back. "And now, she's really never coming back. She was murdered! With that orange bandana that Jerry called to tell you about."

Reaching over, Grampy covered both of my hands with his own. "Chare-bear, I'm so sorry."

Jinx leaped up and curled into a ball in my lap, sensing I needed something warm and fuzzy to combat the cold, hollow feeling I had inside. A few of the tears that I'd been holding back trickled down my cheeks. "In my store, Grampy! While I was there. How awful is that? I feel terrible."

"It is awful, but it isn't your fault," he said firmly, squeezing my fingers. "And there wasn't anything you could do about it. Thank God you didn't have time to try to intervene, or someone might have hurt you too."

Pulling my hands away, I dried my eyes and blew my nose on a napkin. "You're right. That doesn't make me feel any better." I chucked the last bite of brownie in my mouth. "The chocolate helps a little though." I smiled. "And the listening ears. Thanks, Grampy."

"Anytime, Chare-bear. Anytime."

***

The next morning, I decided to stay home from church. I wasn't ready to answer a lot of questions about Serena's death if the news had gotten around. After making a massive stack of chocolate chip pancakes for myself and Grampy, I killed time by cleaning the bathrooms, cleaning the living room, and reorganizing my closet. Not to mention trying not to trip over Jinx during all of the above as my oh-so-considerate cat chose whatever room I was working in to lie in the middle of the floor and take a nap.

"There's a perfectly good rug in the living room," I said to Jinx as I nudged him with my toe. "Do you really need to sleep in the middle of the hallway?" Stretching, the kooky kitty scooted over two inches and resumed napping. I'd never even met a cat who wasn't afraid of the vacuum before, but

Jinx simply ignored it. We continued that little dance most of the morning.

I also made a list of all the things that needed to get done before my parents came into town for Thanksgiving. Basically, I tried really hard to burn off all the nervous energy accumulating from thinking about my upcoming lunch with Detective Sota.

It didn't work. At half past noon when I walked outside and down the drive to my car, I still had butterflies. But, hey, at least the house was clean.

Climbing into my white Toyota RAV4, I told myself to get a grip and drove the short distance from my rural neighborhood to the center of downtown, the area we all called restaurant row.

Restaurant row had some of everything from diners to buffets to chain restaurants and even some fancy-schmancy steakhouses and Italian restaurants. Pizza Palace definitely took a top three spot in my favorites list though, so clearly Detective Sota had good taste.

Parking in the lot, I pulled down the visor mirror and gave myself a stern, no-nonsense glare to send the butterflies on their way once and for all. Everybody has to eat; Detective Sota was probably just being nice by not making me come to the station to retrieve the keys. Then again, maybe he asked me to meet him here just to keep me far away from his work. Remembering my first trip to the station last month and my accidental barging into the employee and prisoner only area, I grimaced. Snapping the visor shut, I headed inside.

Pizza Palace was designed to have two turret-style seating areas: round booths tucked into two round, brick alcoves on each side of the restaurant. The regular floor seating didn't skip out on the fun, though. Each table had dry-erase mazes with damsels in distress that needed saving or dungeons that needed escaping. Kids and adults alike took pleasure in scribbling all over the table while they waited on their food.

Being a Sunday, the place was jam-packed with families. I spotted Detective Sota at the front of the line to order as I took my place at the back. I waved to let him know I saw him as he sought a table.

"Welcome to Pizza Palace," said a perky, pink-dressed teen behind the counter. The pink-jeweled plastic tiara on her head made me smile. I bet a lot of little girls were jealous of her tiara.

"Hi," I said. "I'd like four Dairy Farmer slices please."

"And to drink?"

"A cup from the well is fine," I said, giving the name for a glass of water. Some people might think Pizza Palace went overboard with their palace theme by naming plain food and drink strangely. I found it charming.

"Good afternoon, Detective Sota," I said as I reached the table near the door where he was sitting.

"I'm off-duty right now." He smiled. "You can call me Deegan. Thanks for joining me."

"Oh, ok. I'm Charity. Well, duh, I guess you know that." The first stirrings of those pesky butterflies started in my stomach. Now he'd gone and thrown me off-balance. I searched for something to say. "So, you like the Pizza Palace, huh?"

"I've never been here before, actually."

"Really? It's one of my favorites! I can't believe you've never had it. Which pizza did you get? They're all pretty good. Well, except I can't abide pineapple on my pizza so Royal Page is out, and who would want to eat something called Dragon's Breath, right? What made you pick this place today? Are you such a great detective that you knew it was my favorite?" I paused my ridiculous rambling when I saw a smirk playing across Deegan's lips.

"To answer your last question, a guy from work recommended it to me a few weeks ago. And as for which pizza I got, well, I couldn't pass up something named Dragon's Breath, actually." His smirk turned into a grin accompanied by a wink.

My face heated, whether from embarrassment or a blush I was too cowardly to examine.

A waitress, a princess garbed in purple, brought our slices. Sure enough, six slices of supreme everything were on Deegan's plate. No, thanks; I'd stick to my cheese pizza any day. We munched our way through several bites before I broke the silence.

"I'm not a suspect this time, am I? Do you have any suspects?" I waited as he took a drink before answering me.

"No, you're not a suspect. Too many witnesses placed you in the main part of the store the whole time. Plus, no long blonde hairs were found on the victim this time to tie you to the crime. Also, no, I will not discuss an ongoing investigation with you." He chewed thoughtfully on another bite of pizza, then said, "However, I was hoping maybe you'd noticed if anyone was acting abnormal, or if someone other than Serena disappeared for a long time."

This lunch was just about picking my brain, then? I ate another bite of pizza, then wiped my hands. Fine. Maybe if I told him anything I could think of, he'd slip up and share something with me in return. Plus, I mean, obviously I wanted the murderer caught. If telling him who was where and when last night could prove helpful, how could I say no?

"Okay, first of all, let me clarify that my hair is not blonde. It's light, light, light, light brown." I ignored the raise of his brows and the speculative look he sent my mass of what some people said was almost white hair. Light, light, light, light brown is my story and I'm sticking to it. "Just let me try to remember some of the details while we eat and then I'll be happy to share anything I've thought of." I smiled sweetly. Hopefully, that would also give me time to figure out how to weasel some information out of him.

"Fair enough."

I finished my pizza while Deegan still had one more slice to go. Picking up the dry-erase marker from the table, I scooted to the corner where there was blank space away from the maze and doodled while I talked. Rectangles for tables, initials for people as I named them.

After listing everyone who came to craft night, I put big circles around the people who got up or were not in their seats after Serena said she was going to the restroom. "Jenny, obviously, since she found the body. Kira because she came back into the room while Jenny was freaking out. Bill got up once to use the restroom while I was still helping his wife, Lola browsed the store because she finished her wreath a little before the others." I stopped myself from chewing on the dry-erase marker, just barely. Bad habit. "Honestly, I couldn't tell you if anyone else was up and around because Dana Steiger required a lot of attention."

Deegan pulled out his cell and snapped a picture of my little table art.

"Thanks. What about Serena, how did she seem? Did you notice any arguments with anyone?"

"Well, she really seemed annoyed with Dana." I closed my eyes, trying to recall the evening in more detail. "Wait! She snapped at Kira when she wouldn't work on her wreath, something about Day of the Dead not being a holiday she decorated for and that maybe Kira wasn't in the right spot. Bunny, Kira's grandmother, seemed upset at that but she just kept on working and talking. And then Jenny and Serena did a lot of whispering. I've no idea what it was about but Jenny looked pretty irritated. I assumed it was regular frustrations with a boss, the kind anyone has." I shrugged, opening my eyes. "That's why I'm my own boss, so I only have to be frustrated at myself."

Deegan laughed. "I could stand to be without a boss every once in a while."

"I just can't believe someone who was there to make a turkey wreath for Thanksgiving would kill Serena. Is there any chance it was a stranger who snuck in and killed her?" I asked, doing my best to sound nonchalant.

"I meant it when I said I can't discuss the case, you know?" Deegan shook his head, smirk flipping to a frown. "Charity, I hope you aren't thinking of trying to figure out who the killer is like you tried to do during the Halloween murder."

The maze on the table, one I'd completed at least a dozen times, suddenly required a vast amount of concentration as I led the damsel around the courtyard and out a back exit in the wall to avoid a dragon near the drawbridge. From the corner of my eye, I saw Deegan's frown deepen.

"Charity?"

"Hmm? No searching for the killer, yep, got it." Slurp. "I'm going to get more water. You want anything?"

Checking his watch, Deegan shook his head. "No, thanks. I should probably get going." As he stood, he touched my arm. "Charity, really. This person, whoever they are, killed Serena when a store full of witnesses could have heard or stumbled upon them by accident at any moment. The killer was intentional and strangulation takes strength. Not someone to be trifled with or underestimated, even if you think nobody in that room seemed like they could be a threat." He paused, weighing his next words. "There was no sign of a break-in. The back door was locked from the inside."

Chill bumps sprang to life up and down my arms, that revelation stealing all hope it was a random stranger. Dread spread so quickly through me I didn't even have time to gloat that he'd given me some information after all. Gulping, I nodded in acknowledgement, but Deegan was already walking away.

Four

Tapping my fingers on my steering wheel, I debated the merits of my new plan. The building in front of me was constructed of red brick. Black shades were drawn over the windows. Sandwiched between a bright yellow deli and a nauseatingly pink pet salon, it looked, well, ominous even at three on a Sunday afternoon.

Deegan's words drifted back to me. His description of the killer as someone who didn't hesitate to kill in a place full of people and in a manner that was personal and took force reminded me of my close encounter last month with another murderer. If it hadn't been for my cranky cat catching her by surprise, she probably would have followed through on her intent to kill me after I found out she was guilty.

And so, I climbed out of the car and walked into the red brick building.

The interior was even more stark than the exterior. Gray walls were adorned with black-and-white photos of pebbles and trees. There was no furniture, no plush carpeting. Only long black mats. I winced as a man received a kick to the leg and crumpled onto one of those mats.

"Hello, can I help you?"

Turning, I faced a thin man dressed in black. A gray mustache drooped past his lips and below his chin.

"I called ahead. I'm Charity, and I'm here to sign up for lessons."

With a swift nod, he bowed. "Welcome. You are here for the Krav Maga, self-defense, yes?"

Certain I would regret it but also fearful I would need it, I nodded.

The man smiled. "Follow me, please."

We passed by the large open room of men and women kicking, jabbing, and otherwise hurling each other across the mats and walked into a second, smaller room. The room had less people. Most of them were standing around or stretching.

"The instructor will arrive shortly."

I swallowed and mumbled "thank you" as he departed. Glancing around the room, I noticed two things immediately. First, the class was made up of all women. Second, one of those women was Lola Richards, the woman from craft night who said she'd only recently moved to town, and another was Bunny's granddaughter, Kira.

Kira, eyes closed and moving easily through several stretches, looked completely comfortable in the all-black ensemble that closely matched the mustached man's clothes. Her bangles were noticeably absent. Several other people wore loose, dark clothing. I looked down at my teal and white yoga pants and bright teal shirt. I definitely stood out. Maybe I should have asked if there was a dress code.

Lola, unlike Kira, looked as antsy as I felt as she wiped her palms on her thighs. She kept shifting back and forth on her feet, her bright red hair swaying with each movement. Today she wore it in a long braid that reached just below her shoulder blades.

As curious as I was about both women's presence and about what they noticed last night when Serena was killed, Lola looked like the easier approach. Taking advantage of a large empty space on the mat near her, I casually strolled over and began some stretches of my own.

"Lola, right?" I asked, feigning surprise as I finished touching my toes. "Hi! It's Charity from Sassy Supplies. What are you doing here?"

"Oh, hey. Since I'm new in town, I figured what better way to meet people than to try some of everything the town offers." She shrugged a little self-consciously. "I'm signed up for cooking classes this evening and painting tomorrow."

"That's a great idea." And it was a unique way to meet new people. But it seemed like an odd range of hobbies, all the same. Not to mention how convenient her story was: running out of gas and deciding to stick around town. Is there any way to see if she actually knew Serena? Maybe Becca could help me watch a lot of Serena's videos and see if Lola ever popped up anywhere.

"And what about you?" Lola asked.

"Me?" For a moment, I thought she was questioning me about Serena's murder. Realizing I had been lost in my own thoughts, I gave myself a mental slap and refocused on the conversation.

"Do you do Krav Maga often?" she clarified.

"Oh. No. Never." I laughed. "I mean, this is my first lesson. I've been meaning to learn some self-defense and I guess Serena's murder just drove home the point."

Lola gasped. "She was murdered?"

Several heads turned our direction. Oops. I guess that wasn't public knowledge yet. Not everyone had seen the bandana twisted around her throat like I had. Kira had gone very still and was no longer stretching. Picturing Deegan's official disappointed police officer face when he found out I'd opened my mouth and put my foot in it made me cringe inwardly. That would not be a fun conversation.

"Um. Well." I racked my brain for a way to do damage control. Fortunately for me, a stern woman entered, making her way to stand silently at the front of the class. Multiple people whipped around to face her, bowing with hands pressed together before them in greeting.

Lola and I copied the movement. I stepped away to put a little more distance between us, preparing for class to begin. Hopefully, there would be time to talk to Kira afterward.

"Good afternoon." The woman returned the bow to the room of students. "I am Meira. Welcome! I see many new faces. Let us begin."

For thirty minutes, thoughts of murder fled as I tried to make my body follow the defense stance. We were supposed to do a specific sliding movement with our feet to always remain in the stance. Practicing it was exhausting. Never crossing your feet like you would when walking or running proved to be more difficult than it sounded. Several of the students who were clearly not on lesson one, Kira included, moved on to practice palm strikes and other things I didn't have time to observe.

As class ended, Meira had one more thing to say. "Next lesson, we practice against partners."

Nearly groaning aloud, I shuffled my tired legs out of the room. Lola had vanished before I was able to ask her if she'd gone to the bathroom or perhaps near the storage closet at the store yesterday evening. Luckily, I glimpsed Kira up ahead. Jogging around a few other students, I caught her as she exited onto the sidewalk.

"Kira, hey." I jogged around in front of her and stopped, blocking her path. Her scowl would have made me take a step back if I didn't already know it as her typical expression. How a sweet, bubbly woman like Bunny ended up with a granddaughter of the exact opposite personality, I had no idea.

After a moment of awkward silence, I jumped right into the conversation as if Kira had politely returned my hello. "You looked really great in there at the self-defense stuff. Have you been coming here very long?"

"Few months," she said.

"Cool. Today was my first class. The thing last night with Serena getting killed really made me think about personal safety, you know?"

Cricket. Cricket. Seriously, it was like talking to a statue. Resisting the urge to sigh or shake the girl, I pushed on. "How about you? Are you holding up okay? And Bunny?"

"Fine."

"I was wondering, did you see anyone or anything odd when you went to the restroom? Maybe see anyone hurrying away or hear any noises?" Her eyes narrowed. "It's just the police were asking me, and it got me curious if someone else could help shed some light on things. I hate being nervous and thinking some of my customers might not be safe."

"No. Now, get out of my face." She bumped her shoulder into me and stalked past.

"Be still my heart, a complete sentence," I muttered, rubbing my shoulder and staring after her retreating form. She got the vote for violent personalities in my book. I'd have to come up with better questions before approaching her again.

Five

Monday morning, I arrived to work early. Before I could open the store, the storage closet needed a good scrubbing. There might not be physical traces of death on the floor but getting some soap and water in there would certainly make me feel better.

Once that chore was complete, my stress level lowered slightly. Deciding to make the most of the extra time, I cleaned the bathrooms and tidied up the shelves as well. Rearranging end cap displays and moving some of the Christmas crafts, papers, and fabrics to the forefront provided additional distractions. Time flew by.

Soon, the rattle and bang of the back door signaled Becca arriving at work. The rattle was an attempt to get the door unstuck; the bang was a good swift kick when rattling proved ineffective. We really had to get that looked at.

"Morning," I called out.

"Aigh!" Becca yelped.

I nearly tripped over my own feet running around the hallway corner. "What? What's wrong?"

"You gave me a heart attack! What are you doing here so early? And where's your car?"

"Oh, sorry! I parked out front. I came in to do some cleaning and, since it was still a little dark, I wanted to be near the most street and parking lot lights." Dark circles clung below Becca's eyes. Her dark brown hair was messier than normal, and she tried to hide a yawn. "Are you okay?"

"Sure, yeah. I'm fine." Another yawn belied her words. Becca shrugged. "I'm a little tired. I didn't sleep too great after, well, everything." She waved her arm toward the storage closet before putting her purse in a locker in my office.

I nodded. It was perfectly understandable that Becca didn't want to talk about the murder. I hated what I was about to ask her, but I really needed the help. Plus, if we could help the police figure out who most likely killed Serena, then we could both sleep better at night. As we walked to the front of the store, I said, "Becca, can you remember which customers didn't stay just in the area set up for making wreaths last night? Anyone who went to the restroom or something like that?"

Scrunching up her face, Becca considered. "I think I saw that red-haired girl wandering all over. And Kira went to the restroom, I guess. She nearly knocked her chair over when she stood up. I thought she was a little old to be acting so childish, even if her grandmother dragged her out to make a wreath that she clearly didn't care to do." After a short pause, she shook her head. "I'm not sure about anyone else. I was tied up helping Rita. She accidentally knocked over several spools of tulle, and they unrolled all over the floor. It took a bit to roll them back up."

"Okay, thanks." I hadn't learned anything new, but Becca had given me an idea. If anyone knew exactly who was where, it would be Margo. She was a good person, but she was not known for minding her own business or keeping a single thought to herself. Margo and Rita were twins, and their mother, well, she loved her alcohol. The woman yelled for a margarita in the delivery room and bam, Margo and Rita had names.

My watch showed it was time to open the store. Becca set to starting the computer and checking the cash register while I unlocked the double glass doors. Setting our sale sign up on the sidewalk, I saw three cars pulling into the lot. It seemed we were going to be just as busy today as we were the last time there was a murder. Thankfully, Margo stepped out of one of the cars. Rita trailed behind her, as usual.

I'd always thought Margo's and Rita's natural red hair stood out until I met Lola. Now, their waves and curls looked downright sedate.

"Margo! Rita!" I greeted the long-time customers warmly at the door.

"Oh!" Margo pulled me into a hug. "It's terrible. Horrible. Another body. Are you okay?" she asked, finally releasing me.

"Morning," Rita said simply, giving my hand a squeeze.

Not waiting for an answer to her first question, Margo plied me with several more. "Do the police have a suspect? Are they going to make you go to the police station again? Did someone break in? How did Serena die?"

Not wanting other customers to hear the off-putting conversation, I drew Margo inside and away from the front door. "Let's go to my office."

"Margo," Rita called as she pointed to an aisle, "I'll just grab the things we need for the scarves, if you don't mind."

In my office, I gestured for Margo to have a seat in the extra chair.

"Well?" she asked.

I tried to decide what I could say that wouldn't earn me a lecture from Deegan, Detective Sota, if he found out. "I'm not sure that the police have any specific suspects yet, but no, I wasn't asked to come in for additional questioning or anything."

"Hmm, that's too bad. That detective is pretty hunky if you ask me. I wouldn't mind a little one-on-one chat. Of course," Margo drawled, lifting her eyebrows, "from what I hear, you've already been spending some time with Detective Droolworthy."

"What?"

"My cousin's sister's daughter works at Pizza Palace. She told me you were there on a lunch date. When she described the man, I just knew it had to be the dishy detective."

I couldn't begin to wrap my head around Margo's inexplicable ability to always have the latest gossip, nor could I fathom why I would have come up in some distant relative's conversation with her. Shaking my head at the ludicrousness, I tried to set the record straight. "It wasn't a lunch date. Detective Sota needed to give back the keys to the store. Plus," I said wryly, "I gathered he wanted to warn me off investigating, too."

"Pfft!" Margo snorted. "After you helped apprehend the last murderer in this town? The nerve of that man."

Helped apprehend was a bit of a stretch. I'd only tripped the woman so that she couldn't get away, not to mention out of payback for her kicking Jinx. Still, Margo's opinion should make getting answers to my questions easier, so I didn't correct her.

"Speaking of suspects, did you notice anyone who spent a lot of time not working on their wreaths?" I asked.

Margo leaned forward, revealing far more than I wanted to see down her burgundy and yellow striped dress that, coupled with a maroon lipstick, made her look pale. Really, the woman had the most unfortunate taste in clothing in the whole town. "Now that you mention it, that goth girl, Kira, well she just sat there like a stick in the mud all evening. Her poor grandmother. It must be such a trial to deal with attitude like that."

"Yes, I noticed she didn't seem fond of the turkey wreath theme. What I had in mind were people who maybe got up and went to the back for a while? Where Serena—"

"Oh!" she interrupted. "Oh, of course. Kira did go back to the restroom once, but she wasn't gone long. Then there was Bill. He was up multiple times and gone a while for a few of them. I wondered if I should recommend Dana get him on some bladder control medicine, but then when I saw him whispering with Serena off to the side, well, let's just say shame on that man for carrying on with a younger woman." She tapped a bright orange manicured nail on her chin. "And of course, that new girl. The one with hair the color of a Red Delicious, you know?"

Inwardly, I wondered if Lola would prefer my comparison of her hair to a mermaid or Margo's to an apple. Corralling my thoughts, I latched on to the comment that most stood out in Margo's observations.

"Bill and Serena? Do you mean in a relationship of some sort?" The thought wouldn't even form a picture in my head, it was too absurd. "What makes you say that?"

Margo grinned. "I may have chosen one of those moments to visit the ladies' room myself." She dropped her voice to a stage whisper, even though we were the only two in the room. "Their conversation might have drifted my way. Serena told Bill that it was over now and to stay away from her!"

"That does sound pretty bad." I chewed on my bottom lip. I should have known Margo hadn't finished talking yet. She jumped right back in where I'd interrupted.

"Then there's Jenny, the assistant. She was supposed to come help me with the face for my turkey, but when got finished helping Bunny, the woman hurried to the back. It looked like she was in a rush for the bathroom." Margo's phone beeped. "Oh, that's Rita. She's finished the shopping and says we're going to be late to our hair appointment. Nice chatting. I've got to skedaddle."

I stared at the doorway after Margo left. With as much as she people-watched, it was amazing she finished her own wreath.

Six

As I popped back out front, it pleased me to see that Becca was no longer a jittery bundle of nerves. Ringing up purchases, she smiled and chatted with customers like normal.

Margo's insights revealed my suspect list was growing, not shrinking. I needed to clear some people off it. "Hey, Becca. Will you be all right watching the store if I take a long lunch break to run some errands?" It was barely half past ten now, but sitting and wondering a million things was not my idea of a productive day. Better to get out there and start asking some questions.

Bellisima Brushstrokes was an up-and-coming art studio as well as the only place in our little town that also hosted painting classes. Looking up a schedule on their website had been easy; only one class this morning was beginning at 10:45. It had to be the class Lola would be taking. Conveniently, Viola, the owner, also happened to order her canvas and brushes for those classes from Sassy Supplies. Twisting in my seat, I plucked the yellow and turquoise polka dot delivery bag from my backseat. The order might be a week earlier than we were scheduled to deliver it, but surely Viola wouldn't mind.

"Charity, what are you doing here?" She strolled over as I entered the studio.

Her light Italian accent tickled my ears and brought a smile to my lips. My southern accent was probably equally amusing to her.

"Your order was ready, so I thought I'd bring it on over." I handed her the bag full of miniature canvases.

Easels were set up all along the left side of the room. Several people milled around a refreshment table centered in the back of the room, the walls displaying paintings for sale. Smart.

"How sweet of you," Viola said. "Grazie."

"You're welcome. What will such tiny canvases be used for?" I asked, stalling. Lola's red hair made pinpointing her easy, but she hadn't turned toward me yet. Plus, true curiosity had welled inside of me the moment the order for thirty two-inch square canvases came through.

Movement flitted in the corner of my eye. Lola had finally seen me and was coming this way. I pretended not to notice, listening to Viola describe a painting project next month where the tiny canvases could be turned into Christmas ornaments when they were finished.

"Hi," Lola said as she walked up. "Are you here to paint, too?"

"No, actually. I was making a delivery." I pointed to the bag with the curly-cue Sassy Supplies logo on the front in Viola's hands.

"Oh, that's too bad. It was nice to see a familiar face." Lola said goodbye and went to find a place at an easel.

Viola excused herself to start the class.

Before driving away, I texted Becca to see if she could find any link between Lola and Serena on social media. Since Lola was exactly where she said she'd be, exploring other activities and meeting new people, my gut said her story about simply deciding to stay in town was true. Her presence had nothing to do with Serena.

My next stop was Bunny's house. Her delivery address in my store's database led me to a small retirement neighborhood. Cookie-cutter white houses with sky blue trim dotted the street one after another. Bunny's front lawn was covered in, well, bunnies. Stone bunnies, wooden bunnies, bunny flags, colorful metal bunnies, some giant, some life-size. Even the mailbox had bunny ears. I'd always wondered if Bunny was her real name or a nickname. If it was her real name, she'd clearly chosen to make the most of it in the biggest, most flamboyant way she could.

"Charity!" Bunny smiled cheerfully as she opened the door to my knock. "I wasn't expecting you. Don't tell me I'm finally so old I forget when I order things?"

"Not at all." I laughed. "I just dropped by to chat, actually."

"Come in, come in."

She closed the door behind me. I followed her to the living room, which also had been the recipient of the over-the-top bunny bonanza. Throw pillows and embroidered wall art depicted the fluffy-tailed creatures having tea parties, eating carrots, and snuggling in burrows. I suspected Bunny had made several of them herself with craft kits from Sassy

Supplies. Ceramic figurines of bunnies stood on the coffee table, as well.

Bunny sat down and, choosing a rabbit free chair, I sat across from her.

"What can I help you with?" Bunny asked.

Focusing on the conversation I'd prepared on the way here, I skipped the pleasantries and jumped right in, fearing if I didn't make this conversation quick, I might have nightmares about bunnies for the rest of the week. Not to mention, possibly lose my nerve about questioning the sweet old lady about her granddaughter. I felt horribly guilty for considering her as a suspect, but I had to start somewhere. "I came by to see how you're doing. We were all pretty shaken up by Serena's death, and I worried about you and your granddaughter being upset." There, that sounded plausible, right? I shifted forward a bit, smiling encouragingly at Bunny.

"It was terrible, wasn't it?" She fluttered a hand over her heart. "I'll be honest. After jumping to the conclusion that something happened to Kira because she wasn't in her chair when that woman came in screaming, it was a relief to learn it was that instructor instead. That probably makes me a bad person, but it's true."

"That doesn't make you a bad person. It makes you a normal, caring grandmother. How is Kira?" I raised my eyebrows. "She didn't seem happy to be there. Did she have a problem with Serena?" I clasped my hands together to avoid impatiently tapping my fingers.

Looking puzzled, Bunny shook her head. "I wouldn't think so. She has a problem with crafts, really any hobby in general that doesn't involve that karate or video games, so I wouldn't think she'd ever heard of Serena before." She sighed. "I keep trying to get her involved in things in the community since her parents died, but she just doesn't care."

Wincing, I regretted pressing the subject. The reminder of Kira's parents' deaths made me instinctively feel sorry for both Bunny and Kira. Patting Bunny's hand, I nodded sympathetically. "I'm so sorry. I can't imagine how difficult that is for you."

"Thank you." She swiped at her eyes. "Can I offer you something to drink?"

"No, thanks. I've got to run. I did have one more question."

"Okay." Bunny nodded slowly.

"The new woman at your table, I think her name was Nadine. Did she ever get up to go to the restroom or anything?"

"No." Her forehead crinkled at the sudden change in topic. "She and I talked the whole time, really hit it off." Bunny smiled. "Maybe I'll have a friend for future craft nights even if Kira won't come."

"Maybe so." I stood. "I'll show myself out. Thank you for your time."

"No, Charity. Thank you for coming by. I appreciate it." Bunny reached out and squeezed my hand.

The genuine gratitude in that squeeze left me even more uncomfortable with my prying than I'd began. "Hoppy, I mean, happy to be here for you anytime." Grimacing at the mistake in speech, I dashed away from the beady bunny eyes around the room, down the hall, and out the door.

***

Back in my car, I pulled out my list of suspects. Bunny confirmed she and the newcomer Nadine Boles never left their table. I crossed their names off the list. I also put a mark through Kira and Lola's names. They just didn't make sense as the killers. I'd decided Lola was telling the truth about trying to start over in a new town. Killing someone would put a damper on that plan if she got caught; plus, couldn't she have just left town after the murder since she didn't live here or know anybody? As for Kira, she might have had the strength, but no reasonable motive. Of course, murder wasn't actually reasonable. Still, I strongly felt that I needed to keep looking other directions.

Plugging in the next address into my phone's navigation, I bid the yard full of bunnies goodbye. I pulled away from the curb and headed to Astoria Bed &

Breakfast where Serena had been staying, and where I hoped to still find her assistant, Jenny.

Seven

"What do you mean she isn't here anymore?" I frowned at the man behind the front desk. "Maybe try a different spelling of her name? She's got to be here."

The man's lips puckered in obvious displeasure.

"Please?"

He typed away, probably just hoping to make me stop bothering him more than any desire to actually help me find Jenny.

"There is no Jenny, Jennie, Jennifer, or Jen in the register. As I said, the booking for Serena Jackson was for two rooms and was closed out early this morning." His eyes narrowed. "I assume that will be all?"

"Yes, thanks," I ground out.

Where did our little town even find such a stuffy, untalkative man to work at this bed and breakfast anyway? I grumbled to myself all the way to my vehicle, knowing I was being unfair to the man but not really caring. Didn't the police always tell people not to leave town? Why would Jenny already be gone if the murder hadn't been solved? And didn't she care who killed Serena? I asked myself a million questions on the way back to Sassy Supplies. I'd already been gone longer than planned. As much as I'd like to keep tracking people down, Becca deserved a lunch break

Even more customers came in during the noon hour. I stayed busy ringing up purchases and answering questions, a few of which were actually about crafts and not Serena's death. Things finally slowed down early in the afternoon.

Taking advantage of a lull, I combed the computer in my office for a phone number for Jenny. "Gotcha!" Triumphant, I dialed immediately.

"Hello?"

"Hi, Jenny. This is Charity Basham from Sassy Supplies."

"Oh." A pause. "Yes. Hi. What can I do for you?"

"I was actually calling to see how you are. Losing Serena must have been tough. You weren't at the bed and breakfast this morning when I stopped to offer my condolences."

"You were looking for me?" Her voice pitched higher.

It sounded like she wasn't too happy with that idea, which didn't bode well to getting to meet and question her like I hoped. Thinking swiftly, I said, "Yes. I wanted to drop by a sheet cake. You know, good ol' southern comfort dessert."

"I'm fine. You needn't go through all the trouble."

"I insist." For a moment, the line went so quiet I thought she might have hung up on me. "Hello?"

"Today isn't a good day," she finally said.

"That's okay. I understand." Thankfully, persistence was in my nature. "What time is good tomorrow, then?"

"I'll let you know." This time, there was a definite click. She'd hung up.

With a sigh, I returned to the storefront where Becca had taken up her position at the cash register again. It seemed I couldn't do anything else to find out information until after work. I might as well get busy on something else.

"Did you find anything connecting Lola to Serena?" I asked.

Becca shook her head, dark brown braid swinging across her shoulder. "No."

"Okay." I sighed. It was what I expected, but you couldn't blame a girl for wishing a neon sign with MURDERER OF SERENA THIS WAY would pop up somewhere. The weight of not knowing if one of my customers was a killer grew heavier by the hour.

"I did find something interesting. At least, it might be interesting. I'm not sure." Becca spun her phone around on the counter and pointed to an article.

Leaning over, I read the few paragraphs. Apparently, Serena had been offered a timeslot on network television, an opportunity to bring her DIY Decorating into a much bigger, and likely more profitable, spotlight.

"Wow," I said. "It's too bad she won't get the chance now." It was one more piece that didn't seem to fit the puzzle that was Serena's death. Still, I filed it away in my brain.

"And then there's this." Becca tapped a few more buttons and a new screen came up. A picture of Dana Steiger standing in the background of a book signing by Serena Jackson.

"Now, that is interesting." Helpful, not so much. But definitely interesting. Neither Serena nor Dana had acted like they had ever met before, at least, not that I'd noticed.

On impulse, I shot off a text to Jenny, asking if she remembered Dana meeting Serena before the turkey wreath craft night. The response came more quickly than I expected: Yes. Was a prize winner in a sweepstakes. Future guest spot on an episode.

"Hmm, odd," I mumbled allowed, mulling over the information. Future guest spot? What happens to the spot now that Serena is gone? Will Dana be offered another prize, or was Serena the one handing it out and therefore it disappeared? More questions that needed answers.

"What's odd?" Becca asked.

"Did you get the impression that Serena had met anyone who was here, prior to the craft night?"

"No."

"Me neither. Yet, Jenny says Dana had won a spot on a future episode, and Margo overheard Bill and Serena talking, or possibly arguing, in a way that she assumed meant they, uh, knew each other."

"What do you think it means?"

Rubbing the bridge of my nose, I sighed. "No idea, honestly."

"Do you think you should tell Detective Sota?" she asked.

Thankfully, the arrival of a customer saved me from responding. Should I? Probably. Am I ready to? Not quite. Maybe I could talk to the Steiger's, make a little more sense of what Margo overheard, then present it to Detective Sota if it was anything worth mentioning. With that plan in mind, I slipped a smile into place and got back to work.

Six o-clock finally arrived. Becca swept the main store, and I trailed behind her with a mop, AKA one of my least favorite means of back-breaking torture. Grampy had suggested more than once I hire someone to do the deep cleaning once a week. That idea was sounding better and better as sweat collected on the back of my neck. Once we finished, Becca locked the back door, I locked the front, and we went our separate ways.

"Hey, Grampy," I spoke into the phone minutes later. "Don't wait supper on me, okay? I have a few errands to run this evening."

"Okay, Chare-Bear. You be careful," he said.

In the background, Jinx's aggrieved meow sounded loud and clear. "Tell Jinx I promise to bring home extra treats."

"You spoil this cat," Grampy grumbled. Then, "Hey! That's my chair, furball. What are you doing? No, not my favorite socks!"

I laughed and hung up, easily picturing Jinx's affronted attack on all things Grampy held dear. My precocious pet did not appreciate being ignored or undervalued. I felt a tad bit sorry for not being there to take my own share of Jinx's hijinks instead of Grampy bearing the brunt of it all.

***

Since talking to Jenny was out of the question today, I moved down my list to Dana and Bill Steiger. The sprawling, white clapboard house with wraparound porch and tall oak trees dotting the yard was a regular for deliveries and only a short drive past the outskirts of town. The Steigers owned a few rural acres, and the house was reminiscent of the plantation era. It was always decorated, inside and out, with homemade décor, another testament to Dana's frequent visits to Sassy Supplies.

With no traffic nearby, my knock sounded loud on the big wooden front door.

"Hello," I said when Bill answered.

"Good grief, what in the world did she order now?"

"What? Oh! Nothing, actually. I just stopped by to chat."

Bill simply stared, holding the door ajar but not stepping aside to invite me in.

"Bill, who's at the door?" Dana hollered from within.

"It's Charity," I yelled back the same time Bill said, "Nobody."

"Who?"

Bill's frown deepened, but he caved and opened the door wide to allow me inside. "I'll be in the barn," he called to his wife.

Finding the cold shoulder somewhat odd, I made my way into the living room anyway. Dana sat in a recliner, cross-stitching a pumpkin on a kitchen towel.

"That's very detailed," I told her, pointing at the swirling green leaves by the stem.

"Well, hello, Charity. Come in and have a seat."

I smiled as I sank into a worn, pale pink sofa adorned with pillows and afghan blankets. "How are you today, Dana?"

"Fine, thank you for asking. And you? Are you okay after finding that body?" She shivered. Given the humid conditions of the room, I knew it had nothing to do with the air temperature.

"Technically, Jenny found Serena." It seemed cold to say body instead of Serena, even though she was already dead and gone. "Anyway, how are you? I've just been checking in on everyone who was at the craft night to see if there's anything you need. They say talking helps with traumatic experiences." I hoped Dana didn't question me about who they were.

"I'm disappointed."

"Disappointed?" My brows crinkled. I wasn't really sure what I expected her to say, but it wasn't that.

"How so?"

"Now that Serena's dead, my decorating career is dead too."

"Decorating career?" I echoed. *Does mean the one-episode guest spot?* This was proving to be a very strange conversation.

"That's right. I won a contest to be featured on the Christmas Crafts YouTube Bonanza with Serena."

Apparently, she does. At least she's not hiding she knew Serena.

Dana placed her cross-stitch down on a side table, balling her hands into fists. "Whoever killed her has ruined everything. How am I going to be discovered and whisked away to

Hollywood now? Who else is going to give an old woman a new chance?"

"Wow! That sounds like it would have been a fun opportunity for you. I'm sorry to hear you won't get the chance to be on the show now." She seemed so angry Serena was dead that I knew she couldn't have killed her. I tried to say something comforting. "I'm sure there are other ways you can pursue your decorating career. You could even lead a craft night at Sassy Supplies."

"Really? Wonderful. I've already got a plan for Christmas." She clapped her hands together. "Let me just find my calendar and we'll discuss dates. It may be a two-part craft session. I had it set up to start a series, you know."

"Mmm," I mumbled politely. Good job, Charity. Trying to be nice and suddenly you've booked up multiple crafts next month. Oh well; maybe it would be fun. After assuring Dana that I'd get back to her on the dates she suggested, I excused myself.

"Bill!" She followed me to the door and hollered. "Where is that man? Charity, would you be a doll and send Bill in. I need to let him know we might not be going to Bingo in December, depending on my work schedule at your store."

Stifling a sigh, I agreed and escaped the house. After all, it was just the lead-in that I needed to speak with Bill.

"Hey, Bill?" I rapped my knuckles on the red barn door. "Bill, it's Charity."

A grunt was the only response.

"I'll take that as a come in," I hollered, opening the door. Stepping into the dim interior, I looked around and waited for my eyes to adjust.

"What do you want?" Bill moved out of a stall to the side, making me jump.

The crowbar he gripped had me taking a step backward. I'd never thought the man seemed threatening before. However, in a dim barn, with a possible weapon, and after an overheard argument with a dead woman, well…let's just say I could hear Deegan Sota yelling at me if he ever got wind of my current situation. I feigned nonchalance. "Dana asked me to find you. She wanted to talk to you about next month."

"Probably about that stupid computer channel video nonsense again," he grumbled.

"Do you mean the show she was supposed to film with Serena?"

His eyebrows shot up.

"She told me about winning a contest. Seemed pretty upset about not getting to collect her prize." Bill's comment had seemed pretty annoyed at the thought of the show. Did he not want Dana to do it? And if not, how far was he willing to go to keep it from happening?

Eight

Tuesday morning. Two days until Thanksgiving. Three days since the murder.

With an outlook like that, I closed my eyes, contemplating staying in bed.

"Charity!"

My eyes popped wide open. It couldn't be. It was only Tuesday, after all.

"Charity! Honey! Hallooo." My mom's sing-song voice rang through the closed door.

Apparently, my parents had arrived early for the holidays.

"Just a minute," I called.

Upon my father's retirement from a local bank a few years ago, my parents had promptly retired to a beach in Florida. It had become a tradition for me to visit them for Thanksgiving and for them to stay here with Grampy and me for most of December for Christmas and New Year's. With everything going on at the store, I'd called and told them I wasn't going to make it this week.

"Breakfast is ready. Are you up? Are you eating enough every day?"

And evidently, my mom had decided they should return to Texas to check on me.

Procrastination would get me nowhere. I shoved a pair of socks on my feet and shuffled to open the door. "Hey, Mom."

"Hey yourself." She scoffed, leaning in to give me a hug. "My goodness, you look tired."

"Well, I was asleep five minutes ago." Raising an eyebrow, I waited for acknowledgement of her early morning assault on my ears. Nothing. I waited for an explanation for her arrival three weeks early. Nothing.

"Come on. Didn't you hear me say breakfast was ready? You're wasting away," she said as if she stood at my bedroom door every day.

Following her down the hall, I listened to her one-sided conversation about the importance of breakfast, the disastrous habit of young people to live on fast food, and the general disappointment that nobody sat down to a full family meal anymore.

Southern Mommas. I rolled my eyes. The world could be ending, and they'd be trying to give you a plate of food.

"Charity Belle Basham, are you rollin' your eyes at me?"

I cringed at the use of my full name and hastily shook my head. "No, ma'am." *Sheesh*. It was like I was seven instead of almost twenty-seven. This was going to be a long holiday season.

The kitchen table was spread with mounds of biscuits, a pan of sausage gravy, and glasses of orange juice. Maybe breakfast was a good idea after all. Grampy winked at me as he snatched a biscuit behind Mom's back.

"Charity!" My dad burst through the front door. He ducked his head in the kitchen. "Honey, what happened to your tires?"

"Hi, Dad," I said sarcastically. "Good morning. What are you talking about?"

"Come see." He waved me toward the front door.

Grabbing a biscuit from the table, I shoved a bite in my mouth and followed him outside. Bad decision. I nearly choked on the biscuit seconds later as I gaped at my car. Someone slashed my tires!

"Are you kidding?" I sputtered, wiping crumbs from my mouth.

Staring at the damage did nothing to change it. Finally, I told my parents and Grampy to go inside and enjoy breakfast while I reported the slashed tires. *Too bad we never invested in one of those doorbell cameras.*

"I bet you didn't think you'd be hearing from me so soon," I joked fifteen minutes later when Detective Sota arrived to take an incident report.

He grinned. "Wrong. I've actually been wondering how you stayed out of trouble for this long."

My mouth dropped. "Seriously? That's rude."

"I'm standing here and two of your tires are slashed. Seems accurate." After a quick wink, he dropped his playful expression and pulled out a notebook. "Okay. What time did you notice the tires were slashed?"

"Two minutes before I called you." I sighed. "My parents popped into town early today, or maybe they got here late last night, and my dad noticed this morning.

"You drove your car yesterday and it was fine, then?" When I nodded, he asked, "What time did you arrive home?"

"Let's see, I probably left the Steigers a little before seven forty-five.

I'd guess I got home at eight twenty," I said, thinking out loud. The look on Deegan's face told me I should have done the thinking in my head and answered with only the time.

"The Steigers house? As in Dana and Bill? As in two of the people present during the murder at your store over the weekend?" His jaw tightened.

"Yesss." I braced for a lecture.

"Care to tell me what you were doing there?"

"Not particularly." My best smile and cheerful voice did nothing for the growing thunderclouds on his forehead.

"You were investigating." There was no questioning lilt to the words; he was making a statement.

Hoping to defuse the conversation, I tried to explain. "Deegan, listen. I wasn't investigating. I was just checking in on customers and asking a few questions. If I found out anything, I would have come to you with the information."

"It's Detective Sota," he said icily. "And I believe I told you there was a dangerous murderer among your customers."

"But—"

"It would appear someone likes you asking questions even less than I do, wouldn't you say?" He waved a hand at my tires and stalked back to his patrol car.

Standing alone in the driveway, chill bumps rose along my arms. It's early in the morning; I'm tired; I'm hungry. A million excuses why I hadn't considered the possibility that the tire slashing wasn't a prank. That it might be a warning to back off my questions. Of course, Detective Deegan Sota had no problem pointing out the likelihood that someone was after me. Just like he said might happen. I sighed as he drove away.

Luckily, my dad returned outside. He wrapped an arm around my shoulder. "Let's go inside." He led me back into the house.

Mom had a giant glass of sweet tea waiting for me. "You sit down. I'll just pop these biscuits and gravy in the microwave."

At the mention of food, Grampy wandered into the room, grabbed a plate, and joined me at the table. Dad declined a second helping, instead washing the dishes in the sink and throwing the occasional worried glance my direction.

Eating helped. The sweet tea and imminent sugar rush helped more. "Gosh, Mom. Did you add more sugar to the tea in the fridge? This is like syrup."

"I had to. I don't know how you drink that pitcher of watered-down tea leaves." She frowned and I laughed. My mom took southern to a whole new level. It was probably a good thing she and Dad had retired to Florida and not somewhere up north where sweet tea was practically nonexistent.

Jinx padded over, leaping into the chair next to me, paws poised. One low warning yowl as he stretched informed me that sausage was required if we wanted to keep the chair cushion intact.

"Here you go," I said, feeding him a few bites by hand. "Wouldn't want you to starve and waste away, after all." My fluffy and not-so-small feline blinked at me, as if daring me to repeat a comment concerning his weight.

Once breakfast was over, I helped wash the dishes. I debated the necessity of texting Becca that I'd be late or asking to borrow Grampy's old truck. Borrowing my parents' vehicle would be fantastic, a flashy orange sports car, but I figured they weren't in the lending mood after seeing what happened to my vehicle. In fact, the car was safely ensconced in the garage and had been since they'd arrived.

"Charity, I can't believe you called a wrecker." Dad's statement disrupted my wandering thoughts. "We could have changed your tires."

"I didn't call anyone," I told him.

"Then I hate to tell you this, but someone is stealing your car."

Dashing outside, I banged on the door of the tow truck before they started out of the driveway. My cute car sat dejectedly on the flatbed.

"Help you?" the driver drawled out the open window.

"Yeah," I yelled over the engine. "Where do you think you're going with my car?"

"Police impound."

"Excuse me?" Surely, he did not just say what I thought he did.

The man shrugged, throwing the truck in gear. "Got a call to pick it up and bring it to impound, lady. You can take it up with them."

Them. More like him. "Grampy!" I hollered, stomping into the house. "Grampy, I need your truck, please." Detective Deegan Sota was about to get an earful.

"Can't Chare-Bear." Grampy patted me on the shoulder. "I promised your dad I'd drive him to buy you two new tires."

"I can buy my own tires later. I need your truck." Hearing the whine in my voice, I quickly added, "Please."

"We'll be back after a while." Dad hugged me. Grampy lifted his hands in a what-can-you-do gesture and followed him out the door. Who knew what trouble those two would get into?

"Don't worry, Sweetie." Mom appeared at the top of the stairs. "I plan on driving you to work. I need to pick up some things from the store. You don't have a single decoration in this house besides that turkey wreath on the front door." She waved over her shoulder. "Be ready in a jiff."

Nine

Sassy Supplies had never been so clean in the two years since I'd opened the store. Maybe I was working off some frustration. Or maybe I was avoiding playing twenty questions with my mom about my lack of a boyfriend. Either way, by the time lunch rolled around, every spiderweb had been knocked down, dust bunny evacuated from beneath the shelves, toilet scrubbed, and even the mop bucket washed.

Every time I rounded a corner, I found Mom creating a new display or rearranging an end cap. If she saw me, she'd start bringing up guys from the neighborhood or men she'd met in Florida. And every time, I excused myself to the next task that I said couldn't wait.

"Let's go to lunch, sweetie." Mom picked up our purses and walked out.

Since she was clearly determined not to take no for an answer, I followed her out of the store.

The drive to my favorite pizza place was short, even if the line inside was not. Thankfully, they were fast and we were eating in no time.

"I'm stuffed." Mom added another piece of crust to her stack.

I shook my head. "The crust is the best part, Mom. I can't believe you don't eat it. Thanks for lunch."

"My pleasure." She glanced around Pizza Palace with a smile. "This place really hasn't changed a bit, has it?"

"Nope."

"Oh, look!" She waved to someone behind me. "There's that lovely officer."

I resisted the urge to turn and ignored the fluttering in my belly. "Who?" Surely, fate would not be so cruel.

"You know, that detective who came out to look at your car this morning." She waved again. "Oh, good. He's coming over."

"What?" I hissed.

A throat cleared and uniformed legs came into view as he stopped next to our table. "Hello again."

Still perturbed, I decided to turn this unfortunate run-in to my advantage. "Hello, Detective Sota." I emphasized his title. "I'm so glad to run into you."

"You are?" He smiled.

"Of course. Mom," I said, standing to give her a hug. "You run on home and see if Dad and Grampy are back. If they found tires, they can meet me. Detective Sota here will be happy to drive me to my car. At the police impound. Where he sent it." I bit out each sentence without losing my smile, an impressive feat if I do say so myself.

"He will?"

"I will?"

"Oh, yes. He will." And with that, I flounced outside and let myself into the passenger seat of the still-running police cruiser by the door, buckling my seatbelt to show I meant business. Any other day, I would have worried about getting in trouble. Today, I was more interested in causing trouble. Besides, the good detective had threatened me with arrest on more than one occasion. If he wanted me behind bars, I doubted sitting in his car was the excuse he was waiting on to put me there.

Two minutes passed.

Then five.

My decision seemed less ideal by the second. Not because I was sitting alone in a police car. Not because entering a police car without permission was probably some type of felony. Not even because there was no radio playing in this car, and I wasn't about to touch anything. No, my decision seemed hasty after I realized I'd made the mistake of leaving my mom and Deegan, excuse me Detective Sota, alone together in Pizza Palace. And they were talking. Still.

Finally, ages later, or seven and a half minutes if the clock on the dash was accurate, Detective Sota comes out. Thrusting two boxes of pizza at me when he climbed in, Detective Sota raised a single eyebrow.

"Whatever she said, don't believe it," I blurted.

"What who said?"

"My mother. I'm perfectly happy single. I don't need a date. It hasn't been years since I've been on one, she exaggerates. It's best to just ignore her. That's what I do."

Chuckling, he fastened his seatbelt, put the car in drive, and turned onto the road. I crossed my fingers that we were going to the impound lot and not the inside of a jail cell.

"What if your mom said you're under a lot of stress and you don't normally throw yourself into men's vehicles or speak so rudely to fine men of the law? Should I still not believe her?"

Dropping my forehead into my hands, I shook my head. Open mouth, insert foot, that's me. "No. She was right about those things."

"Don't worry," he said. "She did emphasize the word fine and said she couldn't really blame you for wanting to ride with me instead of her to get your car. Something about raising you to have excellent taste."

"I knew it!" I slapped my knee. "I knew she couldn't be trusted to have one conversation without involving innuendos to my dating life."

By now, Detective Sota was laughing. I relaxed. Surely, he wouldn't be laughing if he planned to lock me up.

A few minutes later, we pulled into the impound lot.

"Why'd you do it?" I asked.

Turning in his seat to look at me, he frowned. "Do what?"

"Why did you impound my car, Detective Sota?" My snark gave way to genuine curiosity. "Did you find something on it? Were you able to get clues?"

He rubbed a hand along his jaw. My attention was captured by the afternoon stubble growing in, making him look more rugged than official. Mentally shaking my wandering mind, I looked into his brown eyes.

"I impounded it to keep you out of trouble." He sighed. "At least, that was the goal. Somehow," he waved a hand at the interior of the car, specifically me sitting in it, "I'm beginning to think that was a lofty goal."

I crossed my arms. "Others might call it high-handed or foolish."

"Probably." He didn't argue. Didn't scowl. Simply scrubbed a hand along his jaw again and looked out his window.

Deciding to cut him a small break, I softened my tone. "I'd call it kind of sweet. Thanks for looking out for me, Detective Sota."

He winced. "We can go back to Deegan, at least when I'm not on official business."

"Sounds good. Now, can I have my keys back?" A small break was a small break, but that didn't mean I was going to let anyone dictate when I could or could not go somewhere. "I've got some tires to replace and places to be."

Instead of handing over the keys, he said, "Let's go take a look at it."

Cars in every age and condition dotted the lot. We weaved our way between sparkling sports cars and crushed, twisted heaps of metal that surely were bound for the scrap yard after their visit here. My car was at the back of the lot.

My eyes bulged. "Are those new tires?" The slashed ones were gone.

Deegan shrugged. "I had my guy put your spare on. The other one came from a car that's getting hauled out of here this week. They don't match, but they'll get you home. Emphasis on the word home." He winked.

Before I could even bask in the happiness of new tires, Deegan switched back to overbearing police mode.

Face serious again, he said, "Whoever you ticked off, I really hope you'll stay away from them."

The problem with that is I have no way of knowing who I ticked off. I mean, other than feeling like I ticked off Bill Steiger. Until I had proof he'd acted on that anger, I didn't want to throw anyone under the bus. For now, I needed to give Dad and Grampy a call and explain new tires weren't needed after all.

Ten

"Many customers?" I asked Becca after coming through the back door and putting my purse in the office. She was restocking the felt supply on aisle nine. The store was pretty quiet.

"It's slacked off a bit today," she said.

Nodding, I flicked through the other boxes on the floor. "I'll take the paints." I grabbed one and headed for another aisle. "By the time we leave early tomorrow, this store will be stuffed full of new stock, and we won't have to do a thing when we come back from Thanksgiving besides rest from our food comas."

Becca's tinkling laughter followed me around the corner, and I smiled. It was good to hear the girl laugh after recent events. After I restocked several shelves, the distractions had worn off. My brain itched to solve the mystery before the holidays began. With Deegan refusing to share how the investigation was going, and so far, no arrests, I had to assume it was going slow. Tugging my phone from my jeans pocket, I quickly texted Jenny, Serena's assistant, even though it was a long shot. Much to my surprise, she answered immediately.

"Yes!"

"Umm." From the end of the aisle, Becca stared at me like I was an alien. "I've never seen you so excited about yarn before. Special project?"

"Huh?" Shelving the yarn in my hand, I laughed. "No, it wasn't the yarn. I got a message I've been waiting on, that's all."

"A guy?" She waggled her eyebrows.

"No. Sheesh, don't you start too."

Becca laughed. "Couldn't resist. I heard your mom after you all morning about getting a date."

Groaning, I finished shelving the supplies from my last box. "I'm all done, what about you?"

Holding an empty box up, she nodded. "Finished."

"Just in time, sounds like." The front door chime alerted us to an entering customer. "I'll go up front if you want to take the boxes to the storage room and break them down."

"Sure." Becca took my empty box as I made my way to the cash register.

"Bill!" I said in surprise. "What brings you by today? Is Dana already browsing?" The older woman wasn't anywhere in sight.

"No, she's at home." Bill stepped closer.

My heartbeat sped up. "Oh? Did she send you to pick something up?" Bill had never come to Sassy Supplies alone, and my brain fought to come up with a plausible explanation. I desperately didn't want to think he'd slashed my tires. Or killed Serena. But my nerves weren't on board with giving him the benefit of the doubt. My hands began to sweat, and I wished Becca would hurry up and come back.

"No."

His single syllable reply shouldn't have made my stomach plummet, but it did. Inching closer to the cash register, I wrapped my hand around a stapler, pretending to staple some invoices. It was the best weapon within reach. "Oh," I said again, stalling. "Well. Okay. What can I do for you?"

"You've already done enough."

Gulp. Here it comes. I flinched as he stepped closer, my grip tightening. The stapler closed on air with a loud click.

"Thank you." Bill put a hand on my arm.

I forced my eyes open, not sure when I'd closed them. "What?"

"Thank you for telling Dana she can come teach a class. She's been driving me wild ever since that Serena woman said she was going to move to the big-time TV position. The move would void the prize Dana won to be part of the DIY show." Bill ran a hand over his bald head. "She's been moping around, moaning and complaining about how unfair life is. I didn't think I could take much more."

"So, you wanted her to be on the show?" I asked, wheels spinning, afraid this thank you was too good to be true after I'd convinced myself he was about to murder me.

"Yeah. It would give her something to do and get her out of my hair." He frowned. "At the turkey wreath craft night, I tried to convince Serena to give Dana a small spot on the new show. She told me it was too late. It was over, and there was nothing I could do about it. Dana was heartbroken when I'd told her on the way home. Anyway, that's all I came to say. Just thank you. You made the holidays happy at our place again. Dana's been in a planning frenzy since you left, just whistlin' and singin' and writing out plans."

"Well." I set down the stapler. "You're very welcome. I'm looking forward to Dana's ideas for craft nights."

Seconds after Bill left, Becca returned from the storeroom. Of course. Oh well, at least I hadn't needed her to come rescue me after all.

"What do you say we close up early?" I asked her. "After all, it's the eve before Thanksgiving Eve and we only work a half-day tomorrow. Might as well leave early today, too."

"Really?" She grinned.

"You bet."

Eleven

Since we closed early, there was plenty of time for me to run home and pick up the sheet cake that I'd texted and asked Mom to bake. In Jenny's text, she had offered to meet me at a park not far off the highway. She said it was halfway between Becksville and where she was staying. I agreed, happy to be talking to the last person on my list. Maybe she would have some insight into Serena since they had worked together.

The clock on the stove showed I still had enough time to sit and drank a glass of tea. I joined Mom at the kitchen table. "Thanks, Mom. I really appreciate you making this." Lifting the lid on the carrier, I inhaled the deep chocolate aroma of cake and frosting. My stomach growled.

"Here." She handed me a covered plate. "Had to make a small, sample cake first. You better taste it," she said with a wide smile.

Maybe this whole parents-home-earlier-than-expected thing won't be all that bad. I plunged my fork into a rich, moist cake oozing with chocolate icing and perfectly crunchy bites of pecans. "Delicious!"

Jinx meandered into the room, pausing long enough to use my ankles as a scratching post before landing softly in the chair next to me.

"I know, I know," I said, losing the staring contest with my piqued pet. "Since I forgot your treats, why don't you ride along with me this evening? We'll stop at the pet store and pick out a new scratching post. That way you don't have to use my legs."

Jinx's look said wishful thinking on that last bit, but he sashayed into my lap anyway, waiting to be taken on an outing.

***

The radio in my car belted some country song hits while I drove to meet

Jenny. Naturally, my thoughts wandered back to the murder. It seemed they never strayed from it, actually. Having dismissed Bill as the tire-slashing culprit, I mentally went over the list of people I'd spoken to. The only name I came up with that I felt certain I'd upset was Kira. Images of her impressive Krav Maga practice flashed through my head. Maybe I should talk with Bunny again.

Lost in thought, I hadn't noticed how quickly the sky was growing dark. I flipped radio stations until I found a news broadcast. Sure enough, a storm was coming. Jinx slept on, curled up in the passenger seat without a care in the world. A quick check of the GPS told me the park was only six more minutes away.

Hopefully, I could hand over the cake and question Jenny before the rain hit.

Five minutes after we were supposed to meet, Jenny still hadn't shown up. Ten minutes. Small drops of rain sprinkled down. Twelve minutes. I tried calling her but got no answer. When rain began pelting the windshield so hard that visibility grew bad and fifteen minutes had passed, I decided to give up. Even Jinx let out a plaintive meow, scowling at the water cascading down the window. Hoping nothing had happened to Jenny on her way, I pulled out of the park and promised myself to check in with her tomorrow.

The rain didn't slacken. "Sorry, Jinx," I said, turning the windshield wipers faster. "We have to postpone that pet store trip unless you want to go swimming through this mess to get in the store." Although I didn't take my eyes off the road to look, I could imagine the glare my cantankerous cat was shooting at me.

Headlights loomed large in my rearview mirror. Before I even knew what was happening, the speeding vehicle slammed into my car, creating a crunch of metal on metal and a bone-jarring thump. I gripped the wheel but could feel the loss of traction on the wet roads. Instead of slowing or passing, the car continued to plow into my back fender. My car slid into the opposite lane, thankfully void of oncoming traffic, and then into the ditch. I screamed. A ball of white fur plunked onto my shoulder as Jinx flew toward me. The car tilted then flipped onto the side, the tightened seatbelt the only thing that kept my head from slamming through the window.

For a second, after everything went still, I couldn't breathe. Opening my mouth to gasp for air, I clawed at the object obstructing my face, only to realize it was Jinx's fluffy tail. Peeling my petrified pet off me proved difficult and painful. Once I had him out of the way, I jabbed my finger at the seatbelt button until it finally released. Scared, hurting, and getting soaked by the rain pouring in the door the moment I opened it, I carefully clambered up, out the driver's door and down the side of the vehicle.

Jinx stuck to me like needles in a pincushion, literally, until we reached the ground.

Darkness enveloped the road. The other car was gone. The storm was deafening. Reaching for my back pocket, I sobbed in relief to find my phone. I dialed 911 as fast as my fingers would move.

Dispatch told me to stay on the line as they retrieved my location from GPS data. Headlights crested the hill in the direction of Becksville. The car put on its blinker as it drew closer and stopped. I would have jumped for joy if every muscle didn't hurt so badly.

"Miss Basham," the dispatcher was saying. "An ambulance is on the way."

I barely heard the words as the phone slipped through my wet shaking fingers.

"Hello, Charity," Jenny said.

Twelve

The crushed front end of her dark car, splashed in white paint the same color as mine, didn't register nearly as quickly as the gun pointed at me when she stepped into the beams of the headlights.

"Jenny?"

"That's right."

"But, why?" Bits and pieces rattled around in my brain like loose pieces in a puzzle box. Jenny was irritated with

Serena the night of the turkey wreath craft. Jenny didn't stay in town even a day after the murder. Jenny didn't want to meet with me. The pieces were there, but I couldn't form them into a complete picture. "Why are you doing this?" I asked, waving at the gun and my car. "I was bringing you cake!"

"Oh, please." It was difficult to see her whole face with the lights primarily behind her, but the sneer in her voice needed no explanation. "You figured it out, didn't you? You knew I killed Serena and you were coming here to talk to me. What, did you think I'd turn myself in? Or were you just going to blackmail me?"

"Why did you kill her?" I asked, unable to even form a response to the rest of Jenny's delusional fears. Blackmail? Who did she think I was? Better yet, what kind of people was she used to dealing with?

"She was going to leave me behind. All the work I did, the shopping, the behind the scenes, making her and her projects look good. Building her YouTube channel up until she was famous. And she was going to take her big break and cut me loose." Jenny stomped closer, her hands the ones shaking now. Anger radiated from each syllable. "I tried to change her mind, but she was too good for small-time Jenny once she had that pretty new job offer."

"What good did it do to kill her?" I moved slightly to the right, toward my overturned car.

"The contract was signed. The producers are in the lurch. Don't you know? It'll be good for ratings for the heartbroken assistant to fulfill the contract in Serena's honor."

"You killed her, for a job?" I still struggled to believe small, petite Jenny had strangled Serena. I really had to stop making assumptions about people's capabilities.

"For a career, fame, money to set me up good." She waved the gun again. "It would have been better for you to die in the car crash. Oh well."

I dove behind the car just before she pulled the trigger. Over the rain and thunder, I couldn't hear the bullet hit, but it didn't take much imagination to guess it was in the dirt nearby. Crawling, I made my way around to the back end, and inky black darkness, as quickly as possible.

"What's this?" Jenny called out. A yowl followed.

Jinx!

"Charity, do you want me to shoot your ugly cat before I come find you? Or do you want to come out here so I can quit tromping through the mud?" Jenny's threat was punctuated by a deep roll of thunder.

And something else.

Sirens!

I could hear sirens. Trying to buy time, I hollered, "I'm coming out. I twisted my ankle, so I have to crawl. Don't shoot Jinx. I'll be right there."

And I did start crawling. Around the rest of the vehicle, I moved in an army crawl as fast as I could go. The storm would muffle the sounds. At least, I hoped it would. And maybe, just maybe, the ambulance would get here before Jenny could hurt me or my captured cat.

The sirens grew louder. I risked a peek around the car. Jenny must have heard them too because she was turned with her back to me looking down the road. The ambulance still had at least half a mile to go. Seeing my only chance, I crouched and edged closer. Jinx saw me and began a fresh assault on Jenny's shoulder trying to get down. She jumped, letting him go. As Jinx turned his claws on her legs, I took advantage of the distraction and lunged, ramming her arm with my whole body. The gun flew from her hand.

"Ughh!" she let out a frustrated scream.

I stomped on her foot and shuffled back away from her. The wet grass nearly made me slip. Is there a Krav Maga variation for bad weather?

Jenny tackled me and we both fell. Lights danced in my vision. Not the kind of lights when you hit your head too hard. No. Beautiful flashing ambulance lights. And just behind them, a police cruiser.

I yanked Jenny's hair one more time for good measure, then screamed for help.

The hateful look she gave me as she was escorted to the police car and I was taken to the ambulance made me cringe. It made it easier to picture her strangling Serena, too. Shivering, I accepted the warm blanket from the EMT, happy to see they'd provided one for Jinx as well.

Thirteen

"Are you going to say I told you so?" I asked, standing in the doorway of Deegan's office.

He eyed the pan I held aloft between us. "That depends. What's in the pan?"

"An apology sheet cake for not listening to good advice. Chocolate, in case you're wondering." Thank goodness there had been an extra cake at home. The one in the car was ruined, though I didn't mention that aloud.

The beginnings of a grin flitted at the corners of his mouth. "The good advice being from me, I presume."

With a giant and slightly overexaggerated sigh, I nodded. "Yes. You were right. It was way too risky to go off talking to murder suspects by myself. Even if I didn't actually suspect them of murder."

"Well, in that case, I won't say I told you so." He pulled a fork out of a desk drawer, laughing at my raised eyebrow. "One can never be too prepared. Now, let's see that cake."

Apologies, in general, were tough. But, when Deegan pulled out a spoon and handed it to me, I smiled. Sometimes, apologies were also worth it. Without a plate or a care, we dug into a delicious pan of pecan-laden, rich chocolate sheet cake, discussing our favorite foods and desserts and avoiding completely the topic of murder or investigations.

The End

Gingerbread

&

Gravediggers

Katherine H. Brown

Gingerbread & Gravediggers

Cover image by Canva images.
Book design by Katherine Brown Books

First Printing, 2021

www.katherinebrownbooks.com

One

Christmas decorations adorned every conceivable surface. Ornaments, figurines, bows, garlands. The fellowship hall had them all. The result was quite cozy yet unique; everything coordinated but nothing was a cookie-cutter match of anything else.

I inhaled deeply, relishing the heavenly scent of fresh green pine branches as I tucked them here and there.

"We need at least three more tables." Bunny Neugenbauer crossed her arms, eyeballing the room.

As I draped another red and green garland over the podium, I looked up and followed her gaze. There was indeed space for more tables in one corner, if you didn't mind guests having to turn sideways to squeeze between them.

Apparently, the two seconds of attention I gave signaled to Bunny that I was free.

"Charity, be a doll and go out to the storage building to have the men bring in more tables, would you?" she asked in a very non-optional manner.

"Sure, Bunny," I smiled at the older woman. It had been Bunny who recommended that Becksville Baptist Church hire me to decorate for their Christmas Eve fellowship. There was also going to be a gingerbread building contest. The extra income during the holidays was always welcome so I accepted the job without hesitation.

I left all of my decorations in the middle of the floor, assuming the errand for Bunny would only take a minute or two. Opening the side door, I was shocked to see that it was already dark. Of course, I did tend to forget about the time when working, especially on decorations. Plus, the fact that the sun set before six in the evening during winter didn't help matters either. Sure enough, a glance at my watch confirmed it was only 6:15 pm, regardless of the inky black sky outside.

Light shone from a single window in the building located between the church and the back gate of the graveyard. A cold breeze whipped across my face and I found myself wishing I'd stopped to grab my scarf. Yesterday, it had still been sixty degrees outside.

But this was Texas.

Today's forty-degree windchill with the sun out shouldn't have been a surprise, and the temperatures now dipping into the range of freezing would make for several happy children if it brought around a white Christmas next week. Of course, in a week, it could be back to eighty-degrees again; you never knew.

Sticking my hands in my jean pockets, I hurried across the lawn. A sound reached my ears as I drew closer. With a few more steps, the sound became a voice, low and muttering.

"Hello!" I called out, more than ready to get my errand finished and return indoors.

Rather than an answering call, the voice ceased abruptly and a strange clank sounded. In my rush, I almost didn't realize the noise was coming from beside me, beyond the graveyard fence, rather than from the building now in front of me. The clang garnered a few more loudly whispered words that I'd bet weren't thought highly of on church property. Cocking an ear, I listened.

Sounds of chairs and tables clanking together floated from the storage shed; however, the patter of running feet came clearly from the graveyard. Squinting, I could make out a tiny light bobbing among the tombstones. Cell phone, if I were to guess.

"Hey!" I jogged to the gate. No lock. "Hey, who's out there?" Pushing through, I weaved in the direction of the light. The sound of my shout prompted the flashlight owner to turn the light off. I fumbled for my own cell before I remembered it was inside the church, somewhere amidst the pile of abandoned decorations.

"Aigh!" I didn't even see the gravestone. But I certainly felt it. Sprawled in the grass in the dark, I rolled over and rubbed my sore shin through the new hole in my jeans. Great. Just great.

"Need a hand?"

I screeched and jumped a foot at the unexpected male voice beside me, causing me to ram my elbow into yet another concrete stone.

"Sorry, I didn't mean to scare you. I'm Rex." The man spun the flashlight to illuminate his face.

"Is that supposed to make me feel better? To know the name of the strange man skulking around the graveyard in the middle of the night accosting people?" I hoisted myself to my feet rather than accepting help. More bobbing lights behind Rex put me somewhat at ease, especially when I heard Bill's familiar voice, but my new scrapes and bruises weren't putting me in the friendliest of moods.

Rex, apparently unbothered by my lack of politeness, only laughed. "No, no I suppose it wouldn't make you feel better. However, maybe you would feel better to know that I don't accost women in cemeteries; there are perfectly good coffee shops for that."

"Hmph."

"I'm the new music minister at the church." Rex held out a hand.

I shook it warily.

"Charity? Is that you?"

"Hi, Bill. Yeah. It's me." A slightly dirty, disheveled, banged up me, I started to add but didn't. I was too glad to see a familiar face to complain.

"What in tarnation are you doing roaming the graveyard at night?" he asked, shining his light directly in my face.

Waving the light away, I groaned. "I wasn't roaming. I was chasing. Somebody was out here." We picked our way around the graves while talking and arrived back at the gate without further mishaps. "Whoever it was got away when I fell down." A shiver wracked my shoulders.

"What were you doing out here in the first place?" Rex asked.

"Oh, the tables! Bunny asked me to have y'all bring in a few more tables." The light shining from the open storage building door was a welcome sight. I stepped inside, disappointed that it wasn't as warm as it was bright in the cramped little building. "Anything I can help with?" I asked, pulling my light, light, light, light brown hair – I'm not blonde, I don't care what people say – into a high ponytail.

Bill pointed to a stack of chairs in the back. "You can grab a couple of those. If Bunny wants more tables, I assume she wants more chairs."

Latching on to my remaining decorations like a life preserver when we got inside, I finished with the podium and the makeshift platform in the corner, and the refreshment table in quick succession and wished the remaining volunteers a good night.

I walked to my new SUV, a calming baby blue color after my white car and I were in a terrible wreck last month, gripping my keys a little tighter than necessary. The adventure in the graveyard left me oddly nervous, though I tried to tell myself whoever had been out there among the graves was long gone.

Still, it was with a sigh of relief that I slid into my gray leather seat and pressed the lock button before cranking the car. Tired and tense, the drive home was a long one.

Two

"Charity?" Becca, my wonderful clerk and assistant, stuck her head into my office at Sassy Supplies, the craft store I owned and operated.

"What's up?" I rubbed my aching neck, happy for any excuse to stretch away from the computer screen in front of me.

Becca gestured down the hall. "Your mom is out front. She said to see if you're available for lunch."

"I wonder why she didn't call," I frowned. *Oops.* A glance at my silenced cell phone revealed she had called. Multiple times. "Guess I'd better get out there and go to lunch. Can you tell her I'll be right there, please?"

She smiled. "Of course."

The printer whirred to life as I printed off the latest roster of sign-ups for next week's craft night. It would be the second one taught by Dana. The first was last week, crafting ornaments from pinecones. Next month, she planned to teach a class on jewelry making and it had the most sign-ups yet.

"Hey, Mom." I hugged her. "I'm ready for lunch." Mom and Dad had come to town right before Thanksgiving and were staying through the Christmas and New Year holidays before flying back to Florida. It had proved trying at times to be under the same roof as my parents again, but also a wonderful visit that I wouldn't change for the world.

I buckled my seatbelt in the rental car. "Where do you want to eat?"

"Do you even have to ask?" Mom laughed.

Pizza Palace was my favorite restaurant in town and Mom never turned it down. But when she wanted to go out to a nice lunch, we always went to her favorite place in town, The Tasseled Tea Room.

The lace and doilies, plus the crocheted teapots with the namesake tassels on every table, were a bit frilly for my tastes. However, the proprietress, Mrs. King bought all of her yarn and craft supplies from my store, so I couldn't complain. In fact, I was always happy to give her a bit of business in return.

We ordered a pot of spiced cinnamon tea. Cooler weather and the holiday season weren't the only reason for the special blend. It had been my Grandma Alice's favorite. Mom ordered it every time, even in the summer.

"What else can I get for you?" Mrs. King still insisted on taking orders herself. It added to the cozy atmosphere, she said.

I smiled up into her face, lined with laugh lines from all of her seventy plus years. "I'd love a plate of your lemon cookies, please. They're the best I've ever tasted." It was true. Not even a fan of lemon, even I had to admit eating those cookies was almost like drinking a glass of lemonade, the perfect amount of tart and sweet.

"Cucumber sandwiches for me." Mom handed over the menus. "Stop back by and chat if you get a break, ok?" she asked Mrs. King.

"Of course, dearie."

Over sandwiches and cookies, mom and I chatted about everything and nothing. Dad and Grampy wanting to cut down our own tree one year soon. People who were entering the gingerbread building contest, Mom included. And of course, her million suggestions for cleaning cat fur off everything in the house. Apparently, she and Jinx weren't exactly best buddies during this extended stay. According to Mom, my cheeky cat was constantly laying on her pillow, her side of the bed, or pulling only her clothes from hangers in the closet, goodness only knows how, to bat around and nap on. Thus, the obsession with cat fur removal.

A quick chat with Mrs. King revealed she would also be competing in the gingerbread building contest.

"You may have some tough competition," I told Mom as we climbed

back into the car. She didn't respond.
Keys still in her hands, my mother stared
vaguely out the windshield. I knew that
look. "What's on your mind?"

Finally, looking at me, she gave a
sad smile. "Would you like to visit
Grandma Alice with me?"

"Absolutely." I nodded. "Are Dad
and Grampy coming today?" Grandma
Alice was buried in the church graveyard.
Mom didn't usually miss a visit to the
gravesite during her visits home.
Sometimes she went alone, sometimes we
all went as a family, other times it was
only the two of us.

"Let's stop by the house and ask
them."

"Okay." I buckled my seatbelt and turned on the radio, sensing Mom wanted to be alone with her thoughts for a time. A quick text let Becca know that I would be late getting back from lunch.

Three

Not only had Dad and Grampy wanted to come to the graveyard, but Jinx had enthusiastically insisted he be a part of the trip, also. In other words, he glared me down. I caved. What can I say?

Mom insisted she couldn't possibly have cat hair in the rental car, so I drove my SUV with Jinx to the church. Once safely inside the graveyard, gate latched behind us, I sat him on the ground. "Don't go getting into trouble," I ordered. With a salute of his furry tail, my pigheaded pet strutted away, wandering amongst the grass and headstones. I frowned. It was highly unlikely he was looking for mice. More likely, he simply intended to remind me who was boss.

"Are you coming, Charity?" Mom called.

"Yes!" My footsteps crunched along the gravel path as I hurried to catch up to my family.

Grampy reached the grave first. He kneeled to place a single red rose at the base of the headstone. "Miss you, my love."

Tears pooled in my eyes at his sweet sincerity.

Mom went next. She fiddled and fluffed her arrangement of silk poinsettias until I was afraid the flowers would fall apart. "Merry Christmas," she whispered. Dad took her hand, helping her rise. They stood bundled together as Mom composed herself.

My turn.

"I'll drink a cup of cider for you, Grandma Alice." Instead of flowers, I propped a small Christmas tree ornament against the poinsettia arrangement. Christmas had been her favorite holiday. Cider. Decorations. Family. Christ. Candlelight services. Gifts. She'd loved every single aspect.

The first two teardrops fell, bringing with them the realization that this first Christmas without her was going to be harder than I'd imagined.

"Mrrrow!"

A distressed yowl cut through my grief. "Jinx!" My eyes scanned the graveyard, but no signs of the white fluffball appeared anywhere. The cry came again.

"I think he's over this way." Grampy walked toward the middle back row of the graveyard.

"Sorry. Sorry." I mumbled hasty apologies to the residents as I hastened through the grassy areas instead of staying on the path. A mound of dirt next to the back fence had caught my eye.

"Mrroww!"

Skidding to a halt at the edge of the oblong hole, I peered down. "Jinx! What are you doing down there?"

"Is he okay?" Grampy walked up beside me. Mom and Dad's footsteps sounded not far behind.

"Yes, it looks like it." Jinx paced and glared. "At least physically."

"Let me reach him for you." Dad laid down in the dirt next to where I knelt. His arms were much longer than mine and he still barely grasped Jinx. I was so glad to have help.

Jinx, on the other hand, wriggled and wrestled away. I watched him dart to the gate the moment he was free, his white tail streaked with dirt and flicking angrily. My peevish pet had clearly had enough adventure for one day. Not that I could blame him. "I told you not to get in trouble!" I hollered. "Don't act like this is my fault."

Turning back to my family, we all stared down. "What's the deal with this hole anyway?" My guess was roughly three feet long and three feet deep, the hole wasn't an ordinary size for a grave. Although. Yep. It was directly over part of a casket.

Dad shrugged.

Mom looked at her watch, uninterested or lost in thought again.

Grampy kicked dirt into the hole. "Don't know, but I say we fill it in before somebody does get hurt."

Grampy and I put all the dirt back in the hole the best we could without a shovel. All the while, I wondered if this bizarre-sized hole had anything to do with the person I'd heard in the graveyard last night. It would make sense. Except, what were they digging for?

Four

Sunday morning, I tossed the covers back bright and early. Christmas Eve! It didn't matter that I was twenty-six years old, an adult with bills, a job, and responsibilities. Christmas Eve sent a thrill through me the same way it had when I was only six.

Jinx yowled grumpily as I jostled him off of my legs to climb out of bed. A messy bun for my hair, slippers for my feet, and I was ready to go downstairs. As expected, Grampy was waiting for me in the kitchen.

"You didn't start without me, did you?"

"Of course not," he scoffed. "It's about time you woke up, though. Thought I was going to die of boredom in the meantime. Now, are you ready to learn this recipe, or what?"

Grandma Alice and Grampy had a special Christmas mulled cider recipe. They cooked it together for the family every year. I'd been begging to help for as long as I could remember, but Grampy had always said it was secret. "Is Mom going to help, too?"

He shook his head. "She told me she has to get busy wrapping Christmas presents."

While I had no doubt that was true—Mom always waited until the last minute so nobody could guess at their gifts—I suspected she was also a little too sad to learn the recipe without Grandma Alice.

Tying on a festive reindeer apron, I clapped my hands. "Where do we start?"

A pile of sliced oranges and several handfuls of cranberries later, the doorbell rang.

"I'll get it." The snap of a recliner told me Dad had been in the living room as he made his way down the hall to the front door.

Grampy and I finished adding ingredients to the large slow cooker. I stirred it all together, leaning forward to sniff the mixture, anticipating the fragrant smells that would fill the house as it cooked and mingled together.

"Charity." Dad joined us in the kitchen as I washed my hands. "Package for you."

"Isn't it Sunday?"

"And Christmas Eve?" Grampy raised a graying eyebrow.

Dad only shrugged. "Kid on the porch said he was paid to deliver it today."

A quick flick of a kitchen knife removed the tape. Inside the small box was a layer of tissue paper. Unfolding it on the kitchen table, I pulled out the contents in surprise. "A Pizza Palace gift card and a candy cane?" I looked to Dad and Grampy who both shook their heads. They didn't know what to make of it either. Flipping over the gift card, there was no signature. It did have a quick note scribbled.

Well, not exactly a note.

Only three words:

Today at two.

"How bizarre."

"What is bizarre?" Mom breezed into the room, her hair still in rollers.

I showed her the gifts.

"And you don't know who it's from?"

"Not a clue." It was so random. I mean, anyone who knew me knew I loved Pizza Palace so that part wasn't surprising, but why send me a gift in the first place? Wouldn't I see most anyone tonight at the church? *Oh well.* I stuffed both items in a small purse, made a mental note to run to Pizza Palace at two, and dismissed it from mind for now. "So, Mom. I thought you were wrapping gifts?"

"That's exactly why I'm down here. They're wrapped." She turned to my father. "Dear. Would you mind helping me carry them downstairs and to the tree?"

My cell chimed as Grampy and I wiped down the counter and table, cleaning up our mess. "Margo wants me to meet her and Rita for brunch. Do you need any more help before I go get dressed, Grampy?"

"Not at all." He pulled me close for a hug, kissing my forehead like he'd done when I was a little girl. "You go on, Chare-bear." He shooed me away, but not before I saw a sadness in his eyes.

This holiday season was proving hard on everyone.

Five

"Hey, ladies!" Margo and Rita, twin sisters, both stood and I gave them a quick hug before taking a seat at their table in Big T's Griddle. "Merry Christmas Eve."

"Merry Christmas Eve to you," Rita smiled. "We ordered you some chicken and waffles. I hope that's okay."

"Fantastic!" Not only did I love waffles, but Big T's—short for Big Texas—served Texas-sized, Texas-shaped waffles slathered in a Southern Pecan syrup that was to die for. "So, what was the matter you wanted to discuss with me?" Margo hadn't been generous with the details on the phone. For the life of me, I couldn't figure out what would be so important, or problematic, that we needed to meet in person. However, for two of my longest customers, not to mention sweet friends, I was willing to come find out. Flagging down a waitress, I ordered a glass of orange juice to sip while I listened.

"We need your help to dig up the dirt on the dirty graverobbers."

I spluttered orange juice, nearly choking. "What?" Surely, Margo was joking.

"Technically," Rita interjected with a soft frown her sister's direction, "nothing was stolen so gravedigger is a more accurate term than graverobber."

My gaze flicked from one to the other. Neither cracked a smile. They were serious. "You're serious." I blinked. My mouth and brain were struggling to process this information. Thank the good Lord the waffles and chicken showed up at that moment.

Shoveling big bites of waffle in my mouth, I chewed thoughtfully. Mostly so that I didn't have to answer right away. After several minutes of eating, I asked the most important question. "Why?"

"They dug up cousin Jake's grave last night." Margo crossed her arms, lips pursed.

"Who's cousin Jake?"

Rita shook her head frantically, but it was too late. Margo launched into, well, a Margo-style story: long, loud, full of additional side stories about her cousin's aunt's sister's kitten, and harder to follow than a trail of invisible footprints.

"Let me get this straight. Your cousin was…a knight? And you feel his memory has been dishonored by having his grave dug partially open?" It wasn't clear who was more surprised I'd followed the gist of the roundabout story, me or Rita who stared openmouthed.

Margo beamed; her red hair swung in front of her face as she nodded. "An honorary knight. Yes."

Rather than try to retrace the part of the tale about how a man in the twenty-first century, in Texas, had come to be knighted, or honorarily knighted, I asked a more relevant question. "Why me?"

"You found the last two murderers in our town. You'll surely be able to figure out who's out in the graveyard wreaking havoc with people's peaceful rest." Margo nonchalantly continued to eat her breakfast as if my participation was a foregone conclusion.

I didn't know whether I was more flattered or frustrated.

Rita fidgeted with her napkin. I caught her eye. "And you also think I should help get to the bottom of this?"

She gave a small, apologetic smile. "We couldn't think of anyone better to ask."

"You could report it to the police." *There! A reasonable solution.* Now, maybe I could get back to Christmas Eve without guilt hanging over me for not being able to help. One look at Margo's scowl and Rita rolling her eyes shot that theory down.

Sure enough, Margo rapidly shook her head. Words tumbled forth before she even swallowed her eggs. "We did that. They were already scheduled on drive-by patrols because of the first grave dug up on Friday night. Fat lot of good it did."

"They can only do a drive-by patrol once or twice a night," Rita explained. "With the holidays, cops are pulling extra security details at stores across town. Others are away on vacation." She sighed. "If this gravedigger is going to be caught, it's a slim chance the police will be the ones to do it."

I knew how important family, however distant, was to these two. They were truly upset over the opening of their cousin's grave. And to be quite honest, knowing the person responsible had been there and gotten away when I heard them on Friday night, followed by Jinx falling into a giant hole, had me a little riled up as well.

I squared my shoulders. "Okay. I'll see what I can do." Using the last bite of waffle, I mopped up the rest of the syrup on my plate and popped it in my mouth. Margo gushed, spewing forth thanks, praise, rants, and ideas all at one time. Even Rita brightened visibly. *Good job, Charity. Now you simply have to come up with a brilliant plan for catching a sneaky, shovel-bearing, gravedigger that doesn't involve sleeping in a cemetery.*

I chugged the last of my orange juice and told my inner pessimist to settle down.

I could do this.

Somehow.

Six

Back in my car, I checked the clock on the radio. It wasn't time for my mysterious meeting at Pizza Palace yet and while not many places were open on Christmas Eve, I could think of one that definitely deserved a visit.

"Good morning, Charity. Haven't seen you in a month of Sundays!" Dolly, short for Delores, smiled as she wiped chocolate covered fingers on an apron. "What can I get for you?"

"I thought I would surprise the family with an extra holiday sweet treat." Dolly didn't frequent Sassy's Supplies, said she wasn't very crafty, but she could do amazing things to a donut. "Do you have anything new?"

It was a silly question, but a necessary one. Dolly kept a special cart in the back with her latest creations. You had to be in the know to get the good stuff.

Dolly rubbed her hands together; her grin widened ear to ear. "Do I ever! Would you like to choose or should I put together a gift box?"

"Definitely a gift box." Not only did I trust Dolly's judgment, I was also a big fan of surprises myself.

"I have the perfect thing."

With my box of donuts in hand, festively tied with red and green ribbons, I returned to my car and made the quick trip home. Jinx greeted me expectantly at the door. Thank goodness I'd brought home some leftover chicken to appease him. Once he was squared away with a snack in the kitchen, I followed the sound of lively teasing to the living room where I found another Christmas Eve tradition in full swing: checkers, hot chocolate, and cheesy Christmas shows playing in the background.

"Who's winning?"

Dad winked at me. "That would be me. Thirty-two years in a row, now."

Mom scowled and slapped him playfully on the shoulder. It was true though. I'd never seen her win a game. The fact that she kept playing year after year was testament to that woman's love for her husband, especially since he wasn't a graceful winner.

"Cornered again. I'll take this one, and this one, and this one." He triple-jumped Mom's pieces with a whoop.

"What have you got there, Chare-bear?" Grampy peered hopefully at the pastry box in my hands.

"If you can get those two to take a break, I'll show you." I motioned for Grampy to break up the time-honored checkers match, then spread a stack of napkins on the coffee table and returned to the kitchen for my own glass of hot chocolate and several plates. My family had assembled around the table, Dad still gloating with Mom pointedly ignoring him.

"Well?" Grampy asked. "I'm not getting any younger kiddo."

I rolled my eyes at being called kiddo at my age, not where anyone could see of course, and handed everyone a plate. I set mine on the table as I reached for the box. "Drumroll, please."

Dad patted off a beat on his legs.

I untied the ribbons with a flourish. The contents of the box did not disappoint. There was a chorus of ooohs and ahs as I lifted the lid.

"Those look scrumptious." Mom licked her lips, leaning in for a better look.

There was writing inside the lid. I turned it to face me. "Dolly even wrote out the flavors for us, along with a Merry Christmas wish to the family." I read off the flavors and descriptions; my mouth watered with each word. "The snowman face is a blackberry and thyme jelly-filled donut, the wreath with tiny gingerbread men on top is a gingerbread coffee cake donut with cream cheese icing, and the last one is exactly what it looks like—a chocolate-glazed donut dipped in crushed candy cane."

"Rock paper scissors for the snowman donuts?" Mom held out her hand. She and I both loved donuts oozing with jelly and there were only two. If Dad or Grampy wanted one, there would be a fierce competition.

"You two take them," Dad said. "Any objections to me having both candy cane donuts?"

"Ick!" If there was one thing that I couldn't stand, it was minty anything mixed with yummy chocolate. "Fine by me."

"That leaves the gingerbread for me." Grampy selected the larger of the two for his plate and carried it to his recliner. "I'll eat this one and leave the other for you three to sample."

***

A particularly loud, and terribly off-key, rendition of *Santa Claus is Coming to Town* startled me awake. I had to give it to Dad, he was jolly and joyful even if he couldn't carry a tune in a bucket.

"Hey! Look who's back with us." Grampy tossed a throw pillow at me.

I stretched and rolled my neck to get the kinks out before I sat up from my awkward position on the couch. "How long have I been asleep? What time is it?" A yawn threatened to overtake my last question but I stifled it.

"A little while." Mom looked pretty relaxed herself, curled up in an overstuffed chair with a blanket and a book in her lap. She glanced at her watch. "It's about half past one now."

"Wow." I rubbed the grit from my eyes. "Wait! Is it really that late?" I jumped up and nearly tripped on Jinx, curled on the rug below. "Sorry." I stroked him hastily then rushed out of the room. "I've got to get ready for my mysterious Pizza Palace meeting," I called over my shoulder.

Seven

Gift card in hand, I strode into Pizza Palace twenty-two minutes later. I hated to be late, so I'd never been one to primp and preen for an hour when I got dressed to go somewhere. A little eyeliner, color for my lips, and a side braid were plenty of effort for this lazy afternoon.

A skeleton staff worked behind the counter, one girl worked the counter and drive-thru. A teenage boy manned the pizza ovens. Customers were scarce as well. Eyes skimming the booths, I saw an elderly gentleman and a mom with two young boys, neither of which I expected had sent me the mysterious gift. Behind me, the door opened.

I turned to observe the newcomer. My heart summersaulted in my chest. Detective Sota smiled guilelessly, looking genuinely pleased. The first time we met, when he was only Officer Sota responding to a call, he'd given me the impression of a statue, blank and unreadable. Since then, I'd had small opportunities to discover his sense of humor and kind, though still serious, personality.

"Merry Christmas Eve, Charity."

"Merry Christmas Eve." I found my voice and tried not to act as surprised to see him as I felt. He hadn't even made the list of guesses when I considered which family or friends might have invited me to Pizza Palace this afternoon.

"I'm so glad you could make it."

I smiled, still collecting my thoughts. He waved me in front of him and we walked to the counter to place our order.

"You're on duty?" I waved a hand at his button-up shirt and slacks, well-aware that I'd almost come in sweatpants and oddly glad that I had taken the time to at least slip on some worn jeans instead.

"Just got off, actually." He led the way to the round turret booth at the back.

I'd never considered Pizza Palace to be particularly romantic. As we slid into the seat, I noticed how much dimmer the lighting was in the corner, the secluded and cozy atmosphere the curved, high-backs created as they blocked most other tables from view. My cheeks heated for no reason and my pulse sped up a tick. *Ridiculous.* I couldn't believe I was getting all worked up over a quick slice of pizza with a guy. It wasn't like this was a date or anything. At least, I didn't think so.

Before my mind could overthink any further, I smiled. "Hopefully it was a slow day at the office," I joked.

"Yes. Other than some complaints about the graveyard disturbances." He quirked an eyebrow.

My smile faded. "Yes, I heard about those."

"Heard about?" He crossed his arms. "The way I understood it, you chased the guy away one night."

"Not on purpose."

"No?"

We paused as our pizza was brought to the table. "No, I was trying to see who was out there. I had no idea at the time that they were digging up graves."

"Oh, that's much better. Chasing unknown strangers doing unknown things in dark places, alone." Sarcasm laced his words, softened by the dimpled smile he gave as he shook his head.

"There were other people around." I shoveled pizza into my mouth rather than explaining my flimsy justification. The fact that there were people in a nearby building but not actually near me, and who had no idea I was outside, when I launched myself through the graveyard gate didn't exactly lend itself to my claim of safety.

"Charity?" A deep male voice behind me interrupted our banter, for better or worse. I was relieved to drop the subject yet oddly deflated. Verbal sparring with Deegan Sota was fast becoming a favorite hobby of mine.

Wiping my mouth, I turned toward the unfamiliar voice. "Yes? Oh, hello. Rex, wasn't it?"

"That's right." He looked from me to Deegan, his wide smile diminishing. "I'm not interrupting, am I?"

Yes, my mind snapped. "Not at all. Rex, this is Detective Deegan Sota. Deegan this is Rex…?" I let the question linger, realizing I didn't actually know his last name.

"Rex Barnhardt." He extended his hand, shaking Deegan's as he finished the introduction. "I've recently been asked to be the new music minister at Becksville

Baptist Church. Mind if I join you?" He angled into the booth without waiting for an answer.

I scooted over, counting to ten in my head. I shouldn't be annoyed. It was Christmas Eve and Rex was here alone; I had no idea if he had any family or friends in town. The right thing to do would be to help him feel welcome.

Plus, making room for Rex had put me far closer to Deegan, after all.

Of course, I was equally close to Rex, wedged awkwardly in the middle of the two.

"You're a detective then?" Rex smiled at Deegan. "Are you investigating the goings on at the graveyard? I hope you take more precautions than Charity here. She was a mess when I found her the other night, tripping over tombstones and such. You should really tell her to stay away from there."

I grabbed another slice and forced myself to chew and swallow pizza to cover the scowl quickly building up on my face. Who did this guy think he was? And I hadn't been that big of a mess. Well. Maybe I had, but did he have to point it out?

Rex chuckled. "Glad to see you got all of the dirt out of that pretty blonde hair."

"I'm not blonde," I spat.

"She's not blonde," Deegan said at the same time.

I stared at him. His face was completely serious but I could detect a tiny crinkle at the corners of his eyes that told me he was remembering our first conversation about my hair color. He'd mentioned finding long blonde hairs on a murder victim. Informing him that my hair was light, light, light, light brown was clearly a memory he still found amusing.

It warmed me to see him keeping that moment between us, even as Rex's furrowed brow and puzzled expression made me want to laugh. He probably thought we were both color-blind. Served him right for inviting himself to our table.

"Okay." Rex shook his head. His number was called for a to-go order.

As he stood, I tried not to show my relief that he was leaving. "Have a nice afternoon."

"See you tonight!" Rex smiled and ambled away.

"Tonight?"

Was it my imagination or had Deegan nearly growled that question? Looking at him, he took a sip of his drink and continued chomping his pizza nonchalantly. My imagination, no doubt. Still, I answered the question quickly. It would suck if he got the wrong idea when he and I were finally hanging out in non-murder-investigation circumstances.

"I assume he meant at the church fellowship and gingerbread contest."

"Gingerbread contest?"

My mouth dropped open. "Don't tell me you don't know about the gingerbread building contest?"

He raised one shoulder in a quick shrug. "It's been a long time since I've been to church instead of working weekends," he admitted.

"Well, you'll definitely have to come tonight." I launched into a description of the contest, how people would be building massive structures or decorations from gingerbread. Having finished eating, I stood to throw away my trash. Deegan followed and held the door open for me to leave. "When the contest is over, they'll need plenty of people to eat the entries, too," I said playfully. "You seem to be a man who enjoys food."

"Says the woman who just consumed more pizza than I did." He winked. "It's a date."

I was still standing on the sidewalk, waffling between offended and excited.

A date!

I had a date with Deegan Sota!

But first, I had to survive the Christmas Eve Krav Maga class and make it to the church fellowship on time. Not to mention, keep brainstorming ideas for discovering the gravedigger's identity before Margo got ahold of me again.

So much for a relaxing afternoon.

Eight

I blocked a particularly wicked kick to the chest, barely, only to have my feet swept out from under me. "Oomph!" Air whooshed out of my lungs as I landed hard on my back.

"Sorry." Lola grimaced, leaning down to give me a hand up. "I thought you were ready for that one."

"How is it that you're already so much better at this Krav Maga stuff than me, when we've been to the same four classes?" I rubbed a hand on my aching lower back. Self-defense class wasn't something I enjoyed, or looked forward to. Like, at all. However, with my recent history of irritating crazy murderers, it was a necessary evil.

While our class was significantly smaller today, it surprised me that six people had still shown up for the regular Sunday afternoon beginner class even though it was Christmas Eve. Heck, I'd considered skipping it myself. Committing to look further into the gravedigger mystery for Margo and Rita had changed my mind on that score. I hated to admit it, but there was a chance I'd run into a shovel-wielding maniac. A girl liked to be as prepared as possible for instances like that.

Unfortunately, the preparedness was hard to come by, as the soreness on my bum attested. "I'm never going to be good at this," I groaned.

"You'll get there."

"That is all for today. Merry Christmas and Happy Holidays." The instructor stood at the door, bowing to each of us as we filed out.

Since Lola hadn't been in town long, I had a suspicion she would be all alone on Christmas.

"Yeah," she shrugged when I asked. "It's no big deal though. I'll grab a pie and turn on the movie channel."

"Bring your pie to my house instead. We'd love to have you join us for lunch." I gave her my address. "Will I see you at the church tonight?" I asked as we were walking to our cars.

She smiled. "Wouldn't miss it."

Speaking of the church, it was high time I headed home to change clothes. I needed to be at the fellowship hall early to double check that all of the decorations had stayed in place.

In no time at all, I was entering the foyer.

"Grampy! Mom, Dad." I called out, listening to locate my family as I hung my keys on a peg by the door.

"In the kitchen!"

Following Mom's voice, I found them gathered around the table. The room, the whole house really, smelt magnificent. The cider wafted through the air as Mom ladled it into deep Christmas mugs.

"You didn't start without me, did you?" I frowned.

"Of course not." Dad grabbed my shoulder and pulled me into a hug as I sat down in the chair next to him. "We heard your car pull in."

"We thought it would be best to have a cup now, since we'll be home late from the festivities at the church tonight." Mom passed a cup to Grampy who passed it to me.

They repeated the action with Dad. Only when all four of us had a steaming mug in hand did Grampy raise his glass.

"To Alice," he said simply.

We toasted my sweet grandmother in silence. I sipped the hot liquid, relishing the warmth spreading down my throat and through my belly. The flavors shined. I smiled up at Grampy.

As if reading my mind, he nodded. "We did good, Chare-bear. We did good."

***

We arrived at the church twenty minutes early to find a whirlwind of activity taking place.

One front corner of the fellowship hall was crammed with tables proudly displaying gingerbread creations of all shapes and sizes. Plaques in front of each proclaimed the names of the entries, but not the names of the entrants who created them. Though I had an inkling of where the delicate gingerbread cookies decorated with gossamer thin icing in the pattern of lace doilies and tea cups came from, many of the others I couldn't begin to guess.

Even my own mother had secreted her baked masterpiece into a box and whisked it away from home for assembly here at church while I was out today.

As we walked along the row of tables, passing gingerbread men, gingerbread trees, gingerbread Santa, a quaint gingerbread village and so on, I kept making guesses.

After the fifth attempt to pry the information out of her, I sighed. Mom wasn't budging.

"I'm not telling," she insisted. "The contest is to be a blind contest and you aren't going to find out a thing from me until the judging is over."

"But I'm not even a judge!"

She didn't deign to respond, instead simply walking away after stating her intention of checking in the kitchen to see if she could help with anything.

Grampy and Dad wandered into a corner of the fellowship hall to join a table of several men who were clearly trying to remain invisible as Bunny hustled and bustled around the room. She was rearranging flowers in vases, straightening table clothes, and calling directions to anyone in hearing range.

I smirked. Smart men.

"Hi, Bunny," I said. "I'm here to check on the decorations. Is there anything else I can help you with before I get started?"

***

By the time I finished a few last-minute adjustments of the decorations and helped Bunny to find someone capable of running the sound system who could help her mic up for the Gingerbread Contest, cars were flowing into the parking lot.

The table of men broke apart. I waved to Dad and Grampy, signaling they should go ahead to the church without me while I found Mom.

Thankfully, the kitchen was easy to locate.

I simply followed my nose.

Delicious aromas even more tantalizing than the gingerbread welcomed me into the overly warm, crowded room.

"The Christmas Eve Candlelight service is beginning," I said. Surveying my normally immaculate mother, covered in what appeared to be flour and oats, I couldn't help but ask, "What exactly happened in here?"

To her credit, she never looked up from the bowl of dough she was mixing, only frowned. "It was a little mishap with a pie, nothing to worry about. I'm making some mini crumbles instead. You go on to the service. I'll try to slip in before too long."

"Don't people normally bake the food before coming to the event?"

Her answering scowl sent me scurrying on my way.

The lights in the sanctuary had already been dimmed by the time I entered from the hallway through the wide double doors.

"Candle, miss."

"Thank you." I accepted the long, tapered white candle from a freckle-faced teen whose bored stare and slouched pose said clearly that he wished to be anywhere else. Stepping into the darkened room, I peered past the candle flame, attempting to let my eyes adjust. It was impossible to make out where Dad and Grampy were sitting when all I could see were the outlines of the back of people's heads against the low, flickering lights.

As I walked slowly forward, a sharp whisper drew my attention to the left.

"Charity."

As I moved closer, the whisperer held their candle aloft, light shining on their face, and I smiled at Deegan. "So, you made it after all."

I scooted into the seat beside Deegan as he inched down to make room for me. We were packed in tightly, but I found I didn't mind. Nope, I didn't mind one bit.

As the preacher opened the Bible to the story of the birth of Jesus, I listened contentedly. This time of year never failed to make me grateful for the gift of family, friends, and my cozy little hometown. It was even more true this year, after the dangers between Halloween and Thanksgiving, that Christmas cheer was filling me up. Even a little gravedigger mystery couldn't dampen my mood and could certainly wait until another day; after all, who would be silly enough to go fooling around in the graveyard of a church packed with people?

Nine

After the service, I returned the significantly shorter candle to the teen at the door with a smile. My smile. He shifted back and forth, frown firmly in place. I wondered if he had a family dinner or a hot date. Or maybe he just didn't want to be holding a basketful of candles for a lot of strangers. He certainly seemed anxious to get away. Shrugging mentally, I joined the throng of people funneling out into the hallway.

"Chare-bear!"

Hearing Grampy, I stood on tiptoe and searched the sea of heads behind me until I spotted his raised hand waving for attention. I waved back, scooting to the side to wait. It did not go unnoticed that Deegan moved to the side with me, by me or by Grampy. While warmth unfurled from my head to my toes, Grampy's reaction was almost comical. His smile vanished, replaced by a suspicious frown, and if I didn't know any better, I'd say he growled when he greeted Deegan.

"Good evening, sir." Deegan held out a hand to shake.

"Officer Sota." Grampy shook hands, longer than necessary in my opinion. You know, that death grip, don't mess with my little girl shake that comes with its very own soul-stare.

"It's actually detective now," I said.

"Mmm." Grampy turned away from Deegan at last and linked his arm in mine. "Don't tell me you're a suspect in something new? Is he harassing you?"

"No." Heat crept up my cheeks. In case the blush was visible, I quickly blamed the crowd. "Let's get out of this stuffy hallway. I don't want to miss seeing Mom's entry in the gingerbread contest."

Deegan may have said the word date earlier, but I didn't know if he'd been serious. I also wasn't going to announce it for public knowledge, regardless.

Ballet boxes were now set up in front of each gingerbread display. Taking a slip of paper, I added it to the box in front of one entry, silently hoping it was Mom's and vowing not to tell her if I'd accidentally voted for someone else's creation.

A microphone crackled, static squeals making several people jump.

"Hello? Sorry 'bout that." Bunny's voice rang out loud and clear. "Come in, come in. Voting closes in the next five minutes so please, vote if you didn't have time before the service and then take your seats."

"Does she mean that literally or figuratively? Because I'd sure like to take my seat and move it into a less crowded room." Deegan's eyes twinkled as he whispered for my ears only.

Grampy and I weaved around chairs and people until we reached Dad. He appeared to be trying to save us seats at a table near the side entrance that happened to have a great view of the gingerbread corner as well. Car keys, pamphlets, and a packet of gum were scattered around the table, giving it an air of occupancy. He quickly gathered them all up, stuffing them back into his pockets as we each claimed a chair.

"Goodness, Dad. Did you run all the way here from the sanctuary?" I asked.

He mopped his brow with a napkin. "Do you have any idea how much trouble I would be in with your mother if we weren't in front row seats for the contest judging?"

"Good point."

Deegan pulled out my chair and I sat. Grampy had disappeared during the five seconds that I wasn't paying attention, leaving his Bible in his chair to save the seat.

"Where'd Grampy go?"

Dad shrugged.

Deegan scanned the room and shook his head, also at a loss.

Odd. It wouldn't be like Grampy to miss out on watching Mom in the contest.

Bunny continued shouting into the microphone and I focused my attention on her. "There will be three prizes," she explained. "First prize will be for best design, chosen by the judges. Second prize, gobble-worthy gingerbread, a prize for the best-tasting creation, will also be chosen by the judges. Third prize will be the crowd favorite and the results will be tallied and prize awarded based on all of your votes."

The preacher, Brother Joseph Hall, joined Bunny on the makeshift podium which was so well-covered in holly and poinsettias and miniature manger scenery that you couldn't even tell it was two tall stacks of wooden pallets pushed together. The decorator did a super job, if I did say so myself.

"I'd like to add my thanks in as well, that you are all here with us tonight. And a big thank you to Bunny Neugenbauer for all of her hard work and volunteer hours to put together tonight's contest."

A smattering of applause sounded. Bunny bowed and accepted the preacher's hand as he helped her down the step to a seat in the front.

"Now, let me introduce you to tonight's judges." Brother Joseph shuffled through a handful of index cards. "Here we are. Judges, when I call your name, please make your way to the platform and let the contest begin! Bunny Neugenbauer, Nadine Boles, Lola Richards, Rex Barnhardt."

I clapped along, nodding as the names were called. The first three were women I knew fairly well since they frequented my store or the craft classes, not to mention having Krav Maga with Lola. Rex Barnhardt's name being called surprised me, considering how new he was to the church.

And apparently, missing. Nobody stood to follow the women to the front.

"Rex Barnhardt?" Brother Joseph called again, tapping the microphone as if the sound might be the problem. "Rex?"

"Sorry!" Rex ducked into the room from one kitchen door, grinning sheepishly. "Here I am."

"Better late than never. And last but not least, Chuck Graburn." Brother Joseph spread his hands wide, his smile stretching to match.

My gaze darted to Dad. His eyes, too, were round saucers of surprise. "Did you know about this?" I whispered.

"Definitely not."

Glancing around the room, I saw him at last making his way to the platform from behind a decorated fake tree near the front.

Chuck Graburn.

Also known as, my very own Grampy.

As he passed our table, he had the nerve to wink. He knew all along he was going to be a judge and the sly man kept it a secret. I wanted to be annoyed but I was too amused and proud to pull it off. If I were still surprising people when I grew to be his age, I'd consider myself lucky indeed.

Bunny picked up a stack of papers and passed them around to each of the other judges. You could have heard a pine needle drop as they moved silently along the row of gingerbread creations, scribbling notes or scores whatever it was they did on those pages.

"I wanna eat cookie!"

The sheer amount of indignity packed into the yell of a little boy sitting in his mother's lap broke the silence, and the laughter that commenced after would have made a stand-up comedian jealous.

Brother Joseph smiled, speaking into the mic once more. "And from the mouths of babes.… I apologize, folks. The contest excitement has me as distracted as a squirrel in a tree full of acorns. Refreshments are open. Please make a line in through the left and out through the right door of the kitchen. An announcement of the contest winners will be coming shortly."

Walking in the kitchen felt like walking into a buffet. Crockpots, casserole dishes, platters, and bowls lined every visible surface. The scents of roasted meat mingled with those of pumpkin-spiced everything desserts. Spotting at least four types of cookies and cakes made from chocolate, I knew I was in heaven. Or in trouble; it could go either way.

"I'm going to need a bigger plate," I said.

"I'm going to need bigger pants," someone joked in front of me.

By the time I exited the kitchen, I carried a plate stacked with meats and a mound of mac and cheese in one hand, an equally sized plate of chocolate cake, truffles, cookies, and a thin slice of carrot-cake, plus a cup of tea precariously clenched between my teeth as I navigated the room shamelessly, albeit without much speed, back to our table.

Deegan removed the cup from my mouth, sitting it on the table as he raised one well-trimmed eyebrow.

Dad simply shook his head. "Tried to eat me out of house and home growing up, she did."

I cut my eyes his direction, but he ignored me.

"You wait until she goes back for seconds." Dad chuckled. "I tried to enter her in the hamburger eating contest every year when she was little, but her mother wouldn't allow it. Said it wasn't ladylike and she wouldn't have her daughter on stage eating like a grown man."

Deegan laughed out loud.

I ignored them both. Besides, there was perfectly good food awaiting my attention. Who needed these comedians anyway?

Delicious. I wiped my mouth with a paper napkin. The dark chocolate and almond truffles were a definite favorite. I was so glad I'd saved them for last.

Before I could contemplate going back for seconds, Brother Joseph stepped up on the platform and smiled. The general thrum of conversation in the room quieted as he cleared his throat.

"It looks like we have our winners." He waved a paper in front of the mic. "Please hold your applause until all three names have been called. Bunny, would you do us the honor of presenting the ribbons."

Bunny stepped forward from the line of judges behind him. "My pleasure."

"Would each of our contestants please join us? No matter who is awarded a ribbon, I think we can all agree that each of you entered beautiful, masterful gingerbread goodies."

We clapped as Mom and the other contestants rose from their own table and stood across from the judges on the platform.

"Without further ado." Brother Joseph opened the folded paper to read. "Best design is awarded to Kira for an outstanding and proportionally flawless gingerbread castle."

The castle hadn't been there on my first inspection of the entries. I made a mental note to go look at it. First of all, castles, who doesn't love them. Second of all, I couldn't imagine Kira and her surly attitude creating something so, well, whimsical. Clearly, I continued to misjudge the girl.

Brother Joseph continued on. "Gobble-worthy gingerbread was a more difficult decision, according to our judges. They did come to an agreement, however. The award goes to Mrs. King for a delectable gingerbread tea party."

Mrs. King blushed. I found myself hoping she would add gingerbread cookies to her holiday menu. They sounded like they deserved a taste in my near future.

"Last, but not least, the prize of crowd favorite goes to the oversized gingerbread ugly Christmas sweater by

Rita." Brother Joseph stepped aside while Bunny passed out ribbons to each winner.

Clapping began and turned loud quickly. Everyone enjoyed a fun contest.

Almost everyone.

On the platform behind the winners, I noticed a pair of contestants pull Brother Joseph aside. A teen girl, fuming from all appearances with arms crossed over her chest and narrowed eyes, stood beside a woman so similar in appearance she could only be her mother. The mother stomped her foot and was gesturing wildly between the gingerbread entries, the winners and the judges. It was apparent that Brother Joseph was doing his best to calm her down when she suddenly snatched the microphone out of his hand.

Beside me, I felt Deegan begin to rise. A glance told me he saw the same thing I did and was preparing to intervene.

"Excuse me. Excuse me!" The woman with the microphone snapped, silencing the applause from the congregation. "This contest was rigged."

Brother Joseph stood helplessly by and I couldn't blame him. What was he supposed to do, wrestle the mic away from her? That was a lawsuit waiting to happen. Instead, he shook his head sadly and tried to shoo the contestants and judges back to their seats. Some heeded his directions, Mom included. She slipped into Deegan's seat, which I hadn't realized he'd fully vacated. He was moving closer to the platform, staying tucked against the wall as he walked slowly forward.

Grampy remained behind, but did slip back to the side of the platform out of my line of sight.

"Who's the angry lady?" I asked Mom.

"A Mrs. Simmons, I think. She and her daughter Kelley entered the contest together."

The teen, Kelley, stalked over to the gingerbread castle. Her mother kept speaking, or shouting. The woman was so loud she probably didn't need the microphone.

"Kira Neugenbauer wins. Big surprise. What was the last name of one of the judges? Neugenbauer. Bunny Neugenbauer, the orchestrator of this contest." She harrumphed. "And as if nepotism wasn't enough," Mrs. Simmons swung a pointing finger to Rex, "the cheat made sure she had an in with Rex. Dating the preacher's nephew, now that's a two-for-one special right there. Nobody else had a shot with the little vixen cornering the votes."

Gasps sounded around the room. Whether people were more shocked at the accusation of cheating, or the use of the word vixen in a church, I couldn't tell. I personally found Rex being the nephew of Brother Joseph to be a bigger revelation than any of the other nonsense being sputtered about cheating. I mean, seriously, Kira made a castle. A whole castle. The prize for design couldn't have gone to anybody else.

Bunny was simultaneously crying and tugging on Kira's arm, holding her back. The young girl looked ready to leap on the woman on the platform.

Rex, I noticed, had a slight flush creeping up his neck but he straightened his spine and moved closer to Bunny and Kira. His light touch to Kira's elbow, her simmering down next to him, confirmed the claim of a relationship between them was most likely true.

Interesting.

Still, I didn't believe for a moment any cheating, colluding, or judge bribing had occurred.

So busy was I watching Kira brush dirt off of Rex's sleeve and lean in against him that I almost didn't see Deegan climbing the steps. He'd made it to the platform.

The sounds in the rest of the room faded to background noise as I bit my lip, watching intently to see what he would do. Things happened so quickly; half the room probably missed it.

Deegan reached deftly around Mrs. Simmons and snatched the microphone from her hand, shoving it quickly behind him to Brother Joseph who moved hurriedly away and began to speak.

Before he could get out more than a sound, Kelley turned around from the contest tables with the top half of Kira's castle in her hands and slammed it into Deegan's back. Kira, not to be held back a moment longer, let out a growl and jumped onto the platform dishing out the fastest Krav Maga moves I'd ever seen her use, the momentum sending Kelley smashing into three more gingerbread designs.

Thankfully, Rex was right behind her. He wrapped both arms around Kira and stumbled off the platform through the closest kitchen door. Mrs. Simmons rushed to Kelley's side and Deegan, with the help of Grampy of all people, managed to usher them into the hallway.

"Did you see that?"

Dad stood. "I'll go check on Grampy."

"I'm going to help cleanup." Mom was already on her way to the platform.

Hmmm. I could help clean up. Probably should, as a matter of fact. However, curiosity got the better of me. I knew between Dad, Grampy, and Deegan, I'd surely get some or all of the details about Mrs. Simmons and her daughter's departure. But nobody seemed to be paying attention to Kira and Rex. Which, of course, was a perfectly good reason to pop into the kitchen and stick my nose in,

I mean, check on them.

Ten

"Knock, knock." I tapped the door frame as I stepped through the kitchen door.

Kira halted mid-tirade and turned, her eyes tight slits daring anyone else to make her angry. Rex continued rubbing his hand up and down Kira's back and I took it that he'd been trying to calm her down.

"Sorry to interrupt," I said. "Are you okay?"

"What do you care?"

At the same time as Kira answered, Rex said, "We're fine."

Deep breath, I told myself. I could be polite for Bunny's sake for nothing else, even if her granddaughter seriously needed a lesson in manners. "Okay. I'd be really upset if someone destroyed a craft or food that I'd worked so hard to make. Kira, that castle was amazing and you absolutely deserved that award. Anybody with eyes could see that, regardless of…anything else." I tried not to look at Rex. Their relationship wasn't my business. Even if he did seem a tad too old to be dating someone as young as Kira.

"Thanks."

Though she said it grudgingly, I was pleased to see her posture relax. She let out a breath and brushed a strand of hair behind her ear, smiling a tad bit. "It *was* the most fun I've ever had at something that Bunny insisted I take part in," she said with a smirk.

An understatement, I was certain. Anytime Bunny brought Kira to a craft night at Sassy Supplies, it had been apparent she was there against her will. Sulky and sour, Kira didn't ever try very hard to actually complete the projects.

Which made me curious. "So, you have a passion for gingerbread then?"

"As if." She rolled her eyes.

Ah, there was the Kira we all knew and tolerated.

Rex spoke up. "Kira is working on a degree in architecture online. Youngest student they've ever had apply." His face radiated pride as he smiled down at her, eliciting a soft blush and genuine smile as Kira ducked her head.

"Wow! That's incredible, Kira. If that castle was any indication, you're going to ace your degree."

A clanging sound made us all turn. A metal pan spun in circles on the tile floor, coming slowly to a stop in front of the door across the room. Whoever had knocked it down was nowhere in sight. Strange. Turning back, I couldn't help but notice the dirt clinging to Rex's shoes as he stepped around me to investigate. Something niggled in the back of my brain, but I was too tired to pay it any attention.

"Well, I'd better be going. Oh! I almost forgot. Mrs. Simmons and her daughter have been escorted from the property. Thought you'd like to know." I waved bye and headed back into the fellowship hall. Taking a quick look around, I didn't see anyone near the second door; the spinning spoon still didn't set right with me but it would have been an odd conversation to choose to eavesdrop on so I shrugged it off and decided to locate Mom. A few lingering church members were helping to clean while a handful of others were finishing up the last of the food on their plates. The majority of the crowd had evidently decided to call it a night after the gingerbread debacle and most of the tables were empty.

Brother Joseph took up the microphone once more. "Thank you everyone for coming and for your help. I want to make sure we all get home to spend time with our families so please, stack the tables and chairs against the walls. Volunteers are in place to come back later in the week and take the extras to the shed. Merry Christmas everyone!"

"Merry Christmas!" we all chorused back.

Whether it was right or not, I chose to interpret that as all of my decorations could also be taken away another day. I found Bunny, still visibly upset but holding herself together and giving orders like a champ, I let her know I'd be in touch in a day or two to come take everything down and back to the store.

"Of course, dear," she squeezed my hand. "Thank you for all of your wonderful decorations. It looked beautiful." She spotted Kira and Rex rejoining the group and excused herself.

"Chare-bear, there you are."

"Hey, Grampy." The quick look I sent over his shoulder wasn't as nonchalant as I'd hoped because Grampy shook his head.

"Your detective left already. Said he planned to follow the Simmons on the sly for a while and make sure they didn't come back to cause more trouble."

Now it was my turn to do some eye rolling. "First of all, he's not *my* detective." I ignored the snort Grampy interjected. "Second of all, 'on the sly', Grampy? Really?"

"Well, maybe he didn't say that exactly. But he did say he was heading out and would make sure those two sore losers did, too."

A twinge of disappointment flickered in my chest. There wasn't time to dwell on it, for at that second Mom and Dad both appeared beside us.

"A judge? You didn't tell me you were going to be a judge." Mom's indignant huff and crossed arms made me want to laugh.

"Last time I checked, I don't have to run everything by you, oh daughter of mine." Grampy winked. "Besides, when Bunny came to me asking for help, how could I turn her down?"

"Puh-lease," I laughed. "You simply couldn't turn down an opportunity to eat all of that gingerbread."

Dad slapped Grampy on the shoulder. "She's got your number, old man." Chuckling, he took Mom's hand.

"I'm ready to call it a night. How about the rest of you?"

"Yep," I said. "After all, we do need to get home before Santa Claus arrives."

Eleven

Feathers tickled my nose. No. That couldn't be right. It wasn't feathers. Opening my eyes, I saw it was a particularly fluffy white tail of a *particularly* annoyed animal.

"Good morning to you, too." I raised an eyebrow at Jinx, my plump Persian cat. He returned the look. At least, I imagined if raising the facial whiskers above his eye weren't such an imposition, he would have. Jinx was full of attitude.

"I'm going," I grumbled.

The going got easier and my mood more cheerful as I remembered what day it was: Christmas! The scent of cinnamon rolls in the kitchen didn't hurt, either.

"Good morning!" I hugged and kissed each member of my little family, happy to have them here with me. "Grampy, are those homemade cinnamon rolls?"

"You betcha, Chare-bear. Nothing but the best on Christmas."

And they were the best. Melt in your mouth, with heaps of cinnamon sugar and a thick, thick cinnamon cream cheese frosting that was melty and sticky all at the same time. I ate no less than three.

We moved from the kitchen to the living room for gifts. As I opened a few toys for Jinx, I remembered to tell everyone that I invited Lola over for lunch. I knew they wouldn't mind. What I didn't expect was for Mom to tell me she'd also invited a guest.

"You invited Deegan?" I yelped.

"Well, of course, dear. He said he didn't have any plans. You two seemed to be hitting it off. Why would I not invite the man to share Christmas and celebrate our savior's birth?"

"Umm, maybe because no matter that innocent tone you, Mother, are trying to play matchmaker and it's a game I have no interest in."

"I would never." She flung a hand over her heart.

"You would and you are." I stomped up the stairs, Jinx's affronted meow warning me that I would pay for his abandonment later.

"Where are you going?" Mom called.

"To get dressed, of course," I yelled down at her. All feelings of familial warmth replaced with exasperation, I counted down the days until my parents went back to Florida.

Out of my flannel reindeer pajamas and comfortably wrapped in an oversized red and black sweater and well-worn jeans, I nodded at my reflection. I looked comfy and relaxed without being completely frumpy. It was understated enough that Deegan wouldn't think I was trying to impress him.

Because I wasn't.

Obviously.

Next, a high ponytail and a thin swipe of eyeliner to complete my look. That was good enough for me.

Back downstairs, shenanigans were in full swing.

Mom was lighting candles everywhere, but each time she turned her back, Dad would sneak over and blow out several of them.

Grampy was teasing Jinx with a mouse on a string and trying to get him to move. Jinx was pointedly ignoring Grampy, the mouse, and the room in general, reigning over the general chaos from the comfort of Grampy's recliner, as usual.

To top it all off, I smelled smoke.

"Is something burning?" I sniffed.

Dad rolled his eyes. "Twenty-seven candles are burning. They're everywhere."

"No." Before I could explain what I meant, the oven timer beeped.

"The cookies!" Mom dropped the lighter onto the coffee table and took off for the kitchen.

Grampy followed.

Dad took the opportunity to blow out another candle and hide several unlit ones behind picture frames.

I could already tell this was going to be quite an interesting Christmas.

Twelve

"Pass me the potatoes, please." Dad held out a waiting hand.

Mom made the most delicious garlic and rosemary mashed potatoes in the world. So, I did what any good daughter would do—scooped myself another helping before sending the bowl down to Dad.

"This is delicious." Lola kept looking at each dish as if she thought they would disappear. "I don't remember ever having a Christmas meal like this. Thank you for inviting me."

"I agree. My stomach and I are very happy to be here," Deegan smiled.

That smile widened slightly when it turned my direction. I didn't answer; I was too busy praying my family continued to stay on their best behavior. So far, so good.

"Our pleasure." Mom nodded. "Please, eat as much as you like. We don't need any leftovers."

"You won't eat this again tonight?" Lola frowned.

"Nope," I said. "Christmas supper is always…"

"Desert!" my family and I chorused, laughing.

Deegan crossed his arms. His mouth quirked up, but his eyes narrowed, a mix of mirth and curiosity playing across his features. "Explain."

"It's a tradition." I told them how, when I was small, everyone always complained about being so full from lunch. "One year, my Grandma Alice just up and made a new rule. Lunch was for seconds and even thirds, but Christmas supper was for dessert. Or dessert was for supper, as the case may be."

"I think I would have liked Alice," Lola said.

"Everyone did." Grampy said it matter-of-factly, but I could see moisture collecting in the corners of his eyes.

"What other traditions do y'all have?" Deegan asked. He ladled another spoonful of brown gravy over a plate piled high with turkey.

"Oh, not too many more." Dad reached for the bowl of potatoes a third time, frowning to find it empty.

"And the best is up next. You're both welcome to join us on a little adventure." Mom looked at the clock on the stove. "We leave in about forty minutes."

***

We pulled up in front of the Becksville Soup Kitchen in two vehicles. Lola and Deegan rode in my SUV; Mom, Dad, and Grampy drove Mom's car.

"Welcome to our next family tradition." I got out, locking the car behind me. "We come here to help serve on Christmas day. The last shift actually has a lot of homeless or down-on-their-luck people still coming in, but volunteers are in short supply because they've gone home to their own meals by now."

"What's that?" Lola pointed to two large stock pots that Dad and Grampy unloaded.

"More mashed potatoes." I laughed. "We'll have to keep an eye on my dad and make sure he doesn't eat them all. Volunteers bring food as well as serve it. This year, turkeys and hams were smoked by local businesses and donated."

"I had no idea the community did so much at Christmas." Deegan's rueful admission surprised me but not as much as his next declaration. "I'll talk to my boss to see if we can get the police department involved for some holidays next year."

"That's a great idea!"

By the time our hour of serving ended, seventy-nine more people had been fed.

Dad shook his head as he placed the pots back in the trunk. "Not a spoonful left," he said sadly.

"Cheer up, Dad. Lola brought Christmas pie."

"What kind is it?" he asked.

"Christmas!" she laughed.

Grampy frowned. "I think he meant what flavor is it."

"And the answer is still Christmas." Lola clapped her hands, delighted at the looks of confusion being exchanged. "Something you've never heard of? Wonderful! I can't wait to share it with you as my contribution to this excellent day."

Dad and Grampy volunteered to load the dishwasher while Mom and Lola arranged all of the desserts on the table. Mom not so subtly insisted that Deegan and I go start a new fire in the living room fireplace.

Certain my face was flaming hotter than the fire was even capable of, I led the way. Deegan followed. I swear I heard a chuckle out of him.

Note to self, uninvite parents from all holidays.

Deegan placed new logs in the fireplace. I added a handful of kindling. It lit with a *whoosh* of hot air that sent me rocking back on my heels.

"Easy there," Deegan grinned. "We don't need you going up in flames."

I fanned myself. If only he knew, if only he knew.

"Your family is pretty great."

"Thanks. I'm sorry my mother invited you over." Deegan's smile slipped and I hurried to clarify. "I mean, I'm sorry if she made you feel like you had to come. I didn't know she was inviting you. I mean, I'm glad you came, I just—"

My phone chimed. *Saved by a text.*

Grateful for any excuse to stop rambling like an anxious teen ten years my junior, I grabbed my phone like a life preserver.

It was a message from Rita.

Margo is freaking out. Another grave dug up. Can you meet later?

I frowned. Another one? On Christmas Eve night? That took guts, what with all the people who were at the fellowship yesterday evening.

Lightning fast, I sent her back instructions to meet me at the church in roughly an hour and a half.

"Dessert is ready!" Mom yelled from the kitchen.

I stood, expecting Deegan to follow me back to the kitchen.

He tugged at my wrist instead, turning me to face him.

"Something wrong?" He asked.

The tips of my long ponytail swung into my face as I shook my head. Brushing hair aside, I said, "Not at all."

Lines crinkled across his forehead as he quirked one brow. "Really? Because you looked like you got bad news."

I sighed, stuffing the phone back in my pocket. "Another grave was dug open last night."

Now both brows lifted.

"Anyway, nothing to worry about now." Now it was my turn to tug. "Come on, they aren't nice people, my family. If we don't get in there not a single one of them has qualms about eating all of the desserts without us."

Thirteen

"You really don't have to drive me."

"I insist," Deegan said, holding open the door of his truck.

Of course, you do. I tried one more time. "Really. Taking down the decorations isn't going to be hard and it only took two little trips to bring them from the store anyway."

"Well, now you can fit everything in the bed for one trip. Plus, it's the least I can do for the hospitality today." Closing the door on me, Deegan put an end to the conversation.

Sighing, I buckled my seatbelt as he came around and hopped in the driver's seat. Trying to secretly investigate an open grave was going to be difficult with a detective dogging my every move. Okay. Maybe dogging my every move is an exaggeration. And I'd be lying to myself if I said I wasn't pleased to spend more time with him.

But seriously. How's a girl supposed to solve a mystery like this?

We chatted idly on the drive over but I was trying too hard to figure out how to lose Deegan at the church to pay much attention. At last, he turned up some Christmas music on the radio.

As we parked at the side of the church, I knew right away that I'd made two mistakes.

First, accepting the ride.

Second, not texting Rita or Margo to tell them I was getting a ride and we needed to wait.

So, there they were. Leaning against the graveyard gate, waving and yelling my name the second I stepped down from the truck.

Deegan smirked.

I racked my brain, dismissing idea after idea of what I could say that wouldn't sound ridiculous or terrible.

The man simply crossed his arms, leaned against his truck and grinned.

"Fine." I stomped my foot. "You got me. I tricked you into coming to the church so you could help us think about this gravedigger and what he might be after." Whirling, I marched, head held high, to join Margo and Rita.

That was my story and I was sticking to it.

Deegan laughed out loud. "*You* tricked *me*? Okay, I see. By all means, I'm happy to help a group of beautiful women out on Christmas day."

He said that last part within hearing of the sisters. Margo fluffed her hair and jutted out one hip.

Somehow, I resisted an eye roll at her jingle-bell covered sweater dress, significantly lacking in sweater material. Flamboyant was understating it when talking about Margo's wardrobe.

Rita patted me on the shoulder. "Good thinking, bringing along the law."

"Tell me how you found the new hole," I said.

Maybe if we got through this fast enough, Deegan would forget all about it while we took down decorations.

And maybe I'd win a month's supply of chocolate chip pizza, while we were on unrealistic fantasies.

"We came to put fresh flowers on the grave," Rita said.

Margo pushed open the gate, walking almost as fast as she talked. "It was the east we could do for cousin Jake. Even painted a little coat of arms on the vase myself," she said proudly. "But before we got to his grave, I saw the next hole. Now, I know what you're thinking. Holes in a graveyard aren't abnormal. And you're right. If somebody died, holes would be normal. But I check the obituaries every day so I can keep an eye out for future estate sales, and there wasn't a single death the last week." She stopped in front of a hole, tapping her foot. "Not to mention, there's already a casket in this hole, too. He's at it again, that slippery gravedigger."

How that woman could talk so much without ever taking a breath was beyond me, but her ramblings never ceased to make me smile. They'd taken a long time to get used to. But as we became friends, I realized that Margo was Margo one hundred percent through and through, which is something that can't be said for everyone these days.

"You're sure this hole was dug last night?" I asked.

Margo and Rita both nodded.

"We walked through yesterday on our way to the contest," Rita explained.

Margo put her hands on her hips. "That's when I realized that cousin Jake needed new flowers. His were evidently disposed of when the grave tender fixed the hole dug over his grave."

"Did you see anyone else out here around the time you were visiting cousin Jake?" It was probably a long shot. If they'd seen anyone else, it didn't mean that person was guilty of anything more than wishing a lost loved one a happy holiday.

Rita and Margo looked at each other. "Well, we did see two people.

Didn't think anything of it at that moment," Rita said.

"Sure did. One was Bunny Neugenbauer." Margo turned, pointing a finger down the same row we were on, only two graves down. "She was going that way. My guess is that large rabbit wearing a Santa hat is sitting on the grave that was her destination."

The bunny certainly looked like, well, Bunny. I'd been in her house once and nearly contracted leporiphobia from it. Okay. Maybe I didn't develop a complete fear of bunnies; that didn't stop them from hopping through my dreams for several nights after seeing them on every conceivable, and inconceivable, surface in her home.

And her yard.

I shuddered.

Regardless of her over-the-top collection of rabbits, I couldn't fathom Bunny being responsible for digging all of these holes. She got around good for her age, but I still imagined that would be a lot more physical labor than she was cut out for.

"Who was the other person you saw?"

Margo glanced around then leaned closer.

I leaned in, too, listening.

Barely more than a whisper, she said, "Rex."

"Really?" For a moment, I was a bit surprised. He was new to the area. Of course, being the pastor's nephew might mean he had family in this graveyard. *Hmmm.* "I guess that would explain the dirt on his shoes," I said absently.

Now it was Deegan's turn to frown. "Dirt?"

"I noticed it while you were escorting the angry contest losers out last night. I went to check on him and Kira. Mostly Kira. To see if she was okay after her gingerbread castle got creamed by that other girl." Explaining made me feel awkward. I didn't want Deegan to get the wrong idea that I might be interested in Rex. I shouldn't have worried. His mind clearly went a different direction.

"What time did you ladies say you were in the graveyard yesterday?"

"On the way to the contest," Margo shrugged.

Rita chewed on a fingernail thoughtfully. "I'd hazard a guess it was near four."

"And you're saying this Rex guy still had dirt on his shoes a little after the contest which had to be, what, three or four hours after he was seen in the graveyard?"

"Yes." I tried to understand what the big deal was; to guess where Deegan was going with this train of thought. And then I gave up. "Why do you ask?"

"It's likely most of that dirt would have shaken loose long before three or four hours had passed." Deegan pointed out.

Not wanting to admit he might be right, I chose to study the ground around the hole instead. There were footprints. Way too many footprints to do any good, but still, I considered it a good observation to make and continued my inspection.

"What's this?" A scrap of paper fluttered, half buried and half sticking out of the freshly moved dirt. I plucked it up and unfolded it. The garbled handwriting smudged with dirt was difficult enough, but the lack of words made it more confusing.

Deegan leaned his head over my shoulder, his breath stirring the hairs at my neck and I shivered. "Anything interesting?" he asked.

"I'm not sure." I took a step away and turned in the pretense of handing him the paper; in reality, I needed a moment to tamp down my racing heart as it beat out its awareness of him all too quickly. "It kind of looks like part of a math problem. But several numbers are crossed out like they were wrong or didn't work."

"Mmm." Deegan concentrated on the numbers a moment.

I was surprised when he pulled out his phone. Never one to let curiosity go unanswered, I peered around the paper.

He was using the calculator. "Are you trying to figure out the answer? Half of the problem is missing." I looked closer. "You have an algebra calculator on your phone?"

Deegan cleared his throat, pocketing the calculator. He didn't blush, but his discomfort was pretty cute as he stuffed the paper in his pocket and brushed dirt off of his hands. "Technically," he said, "it is called a CAS calculator app and yes. I may have been a math geek in school."

"Ah shucks!" Margo's bells jingled as she slapped a hand on her leg. "Here I was thinking that maybe you two had found a clue."

"Do you think the person responsible for digging the holes dropped it? Or is it a random piece of trash?"

"I wish I knew," I answered Rita with a sigh. "Even if it belonged to the person digging, I don't know how it would help us." Whoever this person was, they'd dug up a new spot every single night. Were they looking for something? Someone? Had they hidden something here at some time? Or were they simply going to dig until they found the most expensive looking casket and then do some grave robbing after all? It was too strange for me to figure out, that was for sure. However, the more I thought about it, the more convinced I became that the person wasn't finished yet. And now, I had a plan.

Or the beginning of a plan, anyway.

Deegan's cell rang. "Looks like work. Excuse me a moment."

As he wandered back out of the graveyard to take the call, I told Margo and Rita what I had decided to do. "You have to play it cool though. Deegan, I mean, Detective Sota would probably lock me up for sure if he got wind of anything."

We exited the graveyard and I latched the gate behind us. Deegan clicked off his phone.

"I'm sorry. It seems I have to run for a bit. Would you like me to drop you back off to get your car?"

"No, that's fine. I'm sure Margo and Rita can give me a lift to the store with the decorations and then home." I smiled brightly. Maybe too brightly. His mouth quirked up, lips tightening in the corner as if he were trying to tamp down a grin. And his eyes. His eyes narrowed ever so slightly. It was an expression I was accustomed to from Deegan: suspicion.

Fourteen

Rita apologized again. "I really wish it wasn't our turn to host Pokeno night so we could come with you. Are you sure you won't wait until another day?"

I gave her shoulder a gentle squeeze. "I really appreciate it, but I'll be fine. I can't shake the feeling that tonight is a good night to stake out the graveyard."

Rita sighed.

Margo, on the other hand, was thrilled. "I knew we did the right thing asking you. You'll have this thing wrapped up in no time." She turned to her sister, bells jingling with every move. "Quit being a worry-wart. Charity can snap a few pictures and turn them in. The villain will be caught and everyone can sleep in peace again, including the dead."

I waved goodbye to the sisters, heading in the house to change clothes and say hi to my folks.

"Hello!"

Nobody answered. In fact, the house was oddly quiet.

A note on the kitchen table explained. "Gone to the after-Christmas sales," I read aloud. "Well, at least that's three more people I wouldn't have to argue with about my plans for the evening."

After putting on black sweatpants and a dark gray sweatshirt, I tucked gloves and a scarf into a tote bag in case it grew colder. For my light, light, light, light brown hair, I decided stuffing it into a hat would be a good idea. My stakeout experience might be zero, but my action and mystery movie-watching experience said that blending in with my surroundings couldn't hurt.

Dusk was falling outside. One look at my bright white SUV and I knew I had to stash it somewhere besides the church. It would stand out as too odd parked by itself at the church at night. I didn't want to give the gravedigger any reason not to show up, not if I was going to be sitting out there for hours waiting.

I drove slowly past the church. Not a sign of life stirred.

One street over, I parked behind Bushels of Books, a quaint used bookstore. With the doors locked, I tossed my keys and phone into the tote bag and tiptoed my way across the road. Yes, tiptoed. Sneaking around isn't in my repertoire and the queasy feeling in my stomach told me that it probably wasn't going to become my newfound hobby after tonight.

The flashlight on my phone was tempting, but I would rather not be spotted by anyone so I left it in the bag.

I inched along the back fence and nearly cheered when I got a lucky break. A second gate! I could sneak in this end and not have to be exposed by the lights on the back of the church that faced the gate nearer the storage shed.

With a plan firmly in place, I unlatched the gate. And cringed. The rusty hinges let out a plaintive squeak that sent dogs barking down the road. So much for stealth.

Not wanting to make more noise than necessary, I spread my arms out and sucked in. Squeezing through the gate without snagging any part of my clothing done, and deserving of a reward in my opinion, I breathed out again and looked around for a good hiding spot.

The problem was, I had no idea where the gravedigger would go next. I needed somewhere that faced basically all of the graves at the same time.

Nothing that I had seen indicated that the gravedigger was going in order or sticking to a pattern of any kind.

That left me with limited choices. I could stand here, sit on a bench one or two rows up, or hide behind the really big oak tree in the corner to my right.

The oak tree won the vote.

No sooner had I set down my tote and settled onto the cold ground, back against the wide trunk, then something tapped me on the shoulder.

I screamed but the noise disappeared into a gloved hand.

Not able to register the shushing sound above the panic racing through my blood, I bit down as hard as I could.

The hand let go.

Deegan's face appeared in front of mine and he waved both hands in a surrender gesture.

My mouth dropped open. "Are you kidding me?" I hissed.

"Am I going to have rabies now?" he asked in a hushed voice.

"If you do, it will serve you right for nearly giving me a heart attack, a panic attack, and if I suffered from asthma then probably one of those attacks, too." I slapped his shoulder. "What the heck were you thinking? And where did you come from? Did you follow me?" I narrowed my eyes. Stalking the gravedigger was one thing. Being stalked was quite another.

"Keep your voice down." Deegan picked up my tote and motioned for me to follow him around the tree. Now we were facing the back fence instead of the graves. I opened my mouth to protest, but he simply held up a finger. "Now, to answer your questions. Let's see. I was thinking that you would come here and do something dangerous and that I'd better come and make sure you don't get hurt. I came from right here, in this tree where I've been waiting for you, so no, I didn't follow you because I got here first."

"Are you telling me I'm so predictable that you knew I'd be here tonight?" And here I thought I'd played my cards so close to my chest this afternoon.

"No, I wouldn't say you're predictable. In fact, you're rather unpredictable. That's how I knew where to find you tonight."

As if that made a lick of sense. I sighed.

Deegan grinned, reached into the crook of the big tree, and pulled down a Styrofoam cup.

"What is that?" I whispered.

"That is your hot chocolate." He leaned down and presented the warm cup with a bow that had me wanting to giggle, if only I weren't supposed to be quietly and professionally staking out the scene of a possible crime. Was digging up graves a crime? Anyway, I skewered my wandering thoughts, giggling wasn't an option.

Deegan reached up and produced another cup for himself and sat down, patting the dirt beside him. Needing no further invitation, I crossed my legs and leaned against the tree.

One sip of the delicious hot chocolate, Deegan's knee resting comfortably against mine, stars twinkling above the bare branches. It all was utterly romantic. So romantic, I nearly forgot why we were here until Deegan spoke again.

"I can't believe you came on a stakeout without proper stakeout snacks."

Men.

I rolled my eyes.

Fifteen

I was on a boat but the boat was rocking. There must be a storm because bed was shaking and it wouldn't stop. I felt like I was going to fall out of it any second.

My head rolled to the side and my eyes shot open.

Above me, Deegan had a finger to his lips.

No boat. It was just a dream.

I shivered. We were still in the graveyard and now it was freezing cold.

Plus, I'd apparently fallen asleep on Deegan's thigh.

"Wha—"

Deegan's finger moved from his lips to mine, hushing me.

A sound intruded upon my groggy thoughts as I uncrossed my legs and stretched.

Clunk. Thwomp. Clunk. Thwomp.

The repetitive scooping and dumping of dirt scattered the last tendrils of sleepy haze from my brain.

The gravedigger had arrived.

For a brief moment, I was ridiculously thankful that I wasn't a snorer. Wouldn't that have been awkward if I gave away our presence while sleeping?

I pulled out my phone and switched it to dark mode. With the lights as dim as possible, I typed on my notepad and handed the phone to Deegan.

I'm not sure why I expected anything different. Still, his response of *you wait here* to my question of what we did next was frustrating. Surely, I could do something. Before I could voice, or text, an argument, he sidled around the tree and disappeared in the gloom and gravestones beyond.

Careful to move quietly, I crouched on the balls of my feet and leaned around the tree. After what felt like an eternity of straining my eyes, I could finally pinpoint the person digging about two rows up. Deegan, on the other hand, was much more difficult to spot.

I stared so long without blinking that teardrops began to collect by the bridge of my nose.

Wait! Was that him?

My breath caught as a darker shadow disconnected from one of the taller tombstones. Deegan, I certainly hoped it was Deegan, crept toward the gravedigger.

Then, the unthinkable happened.

Deegan sneezed.

The sound was so loud in the silence of the night that even I jumped.

Startled, the gravedigger spun and swung his shovel.

Crack.

Deegan grunted and dropped to his knees. In the dark, it was hard to tell but it looked like he clutched his head in his hands.

The gravedigger tossed the shovel and took off running down the line of graves. He was making a break for the main gate.

Emotions warred within me. I was dying to go check on Deegan. Was he okay? How hard had he been hit? Did he need an ambulance? Each pounding footstep of his assailant was a ticking time bomb. If I checked on Deegan, he would get away. Could I even catch him? Should I?

From the corner of my eye, I saw the shadow that was Deegan stand. He wobbled, but I opted to take it as a good sign. Split-second decision made, I bolted from my hiding spot and sprinted along the side of the fence. A few more steps and I could cut the gravedigger off at the end of his row. Unfortunately, a sprinter I was not. The person must have caught sight of me. Or heard my heavy panting for air. Either way, he veered and I knew I wouldn't make it to the end of the row in time. Drawing in a deep breath, I pumped my legs harder and when I thought I couldn't go any further, hurled my tote bag at the guy's head.

It flew past his shoulder.

Note to self, don't take up sports.

"Stop!" I yelled. Nothing else was working; it was worth a shot.

He didn't stop. He did look back to see if I was gaining on him. That one turn of the head cost him everything. I winced as he tumbled headlong over a shin-high gravestone, remembering well my own bumps and bruises from the same accident earlier in the week.

Still, I didn't have it in me to actually feel sorry for him.

Deegan caught up to me at the same time that I dropped onto the ground next to the gravedigger.

"Are you okay?" I asked him, pretending for all the world like I wasn't out of breath and dying.

"I'll live. Let's see who we have here." Clicking on his flashlight, Deegan rolled over the guy on the ground so that his face was showing.

"What the heck?" My shock was real. It wasn't Rex. It wasn't even a grown man. It was the gangly teenager who'd handed me my candle for the Christmas Eve service.

"I'm sorry! I'm sorry!" The kid's eyes were wider than a deer in headlights, fear etched all over his face as he held his hands up over him. "I didn't mean to hit you, I swear. You scared me to death. I thought zombies were out to get me or something. Dude, who sneaks around a graveyard?"

I shook my head. "That's what we want to know."

Deegan hauled him up by the elbow. "What's your name, kid?"

"Eric," he mumbled.

"Come on. Let's go to the station and get this sorted out." Deegan held on to the boy while I turned on my own flashlight app and gathered up my bag and the gloves that had fallen out.

"Who are your parents?" I asked as we all started walking toward the back gate. "Maybe I can call and have someone meet you at the station."

"Dad and Uncle Jo are going to kill me," the boy moaned.

"Names," Deegan barked.

The blood on the side of his head appeared to be dry. Still, I imagined his head was throbbing and his shortness with the boy was understandable.

If I had been hit with a shovel, I'd probably be ready to throttle somebody.

"Rex Barnhardt is my dad." As if uttering a death sentence, the boy dropped his head and never lifted his eyes from the ground the rest of the walk.

If Rex was his father, that would make the pastor his great uncle. I understood young Eric's worries, now.

Sixteen

The lobby of the police station in the middle of the night was depressing. I tried to ignore the sticky floor, muted gray walls, and dim lighting. Since the front desk personnel went off duty at six and it was currently very close to midnight, the place was also silent as the grave, no pun intended.

Deegan had insisted on walking me to my car before hauling Eric down to the station to sort things out. He had also insisted I call it a night and go home.

Ha! It still made me laugh to think of his face when I'd told him what I thought of that idea.

"Excuse me? You crashed my stakeout and now you think I'm going to waltz home and forget about everything. Better luck next time."

Maybe not my finest moment, slamming the door to my SUV and driving off in a huff, but really, being bossed around always riled me up.

So, here I sat. Alone. Cold. Tired. And calling back my family who came home and freaked out when they couldn't reach me.

"Yes," I said for the millionth time. "I'm fine. No, I'm not lying in a ditch somewhere, Mom. No. No, nobody has tried to kill me all night, not even all week. My phone was on silent. I'm with Deegan." *Sort of.* "I'll explain everything tomorrow. Yes, I'm coming home tonight but you don't need to wait up."

I hung up, proud of myself for resisting the urge to ask what day they were going back to Florida this week.

My phone vibrated. Seeing a text pop up from Margo was the last thing I expected. Did nobody sleep in this town?

The text message version of a Margo story was no less convoluted than speaking to her in person. After a moment of skimming, I shook my head. Might as well call her tomorrow.

Caught the gravedigger. Will call tomorrow when I have the whole scoop.

Hitting send on the text, I leaned back in the hard plastic chair and closed my eyes, praying Deegan would take pity and loop me in soon.

***

"Sleeping on the job again, I see."

For the second time in twenty-four hours, I opened my eyes to see Deegan looming over me. That smirk he wore, the one I'd started to find so endearing once he moved past using his poker face on me, was now on my nerves.

"What time is it?" I rubbed my aching neck. No way these cricks were going away anytime soon. With a last glare at the unforgiving chair, I stood and stretched.

"It's a little after two. Are you okay to drive home?" Deegan asked.

"Oh, no you don't." I gathered up my tote bag and phone. "I'm not leaving here without you giving me the rest of the story. So, first, you can point me in the direction of some water. And maybe some chocolate. Well, definitely some chocolate and maybe some water is more like it. Anyway, a few calories and all of the details, then I'll be perfectly capable of driving home. Not a moment before."

Deegan's deep chuckle echoed through the empty lobby. "Stubborn."

"I prefer to think of it as persistent."

"I'm sure you do." He tilted his head. "I bet not many people would agree." Shrugging, he motioned for me to follow him down the nearest hall. "Lucky for you, I'm too tired to argue. I think I have just the thing in my office."

The sight of a cushioned chair instead of the plastic, utilitarian models from the lobby nearly made me sigh in relief.

"You can snag two waters from there." Before I could sit, Deegan pointed to a mini-fridge against the wall as he walked around his desk.

I placed one water in front of him before I plopped down in the comfy chair. When Deegan opened a drawer and pulled out two Snickers candy bars, I really did sigh.

The chocolate did wonders. Halfway through the bar, I almost felt like a human instead of a zombie. Too bad it hadn't also worked miracles on my appearance. I took a minute to redo my falling down ponytail before getting to business.

"Did you find out why in the world Eric was digging up half the graveyard?" I leaned forward. "Was he stealing after all? Or does he have some bizarre obsession with death? Is he going to jail?"

"His motives were nothing so sinister." Deegan took another bite of candy bar. "And his father and I decided a math tutor would be suitable punishment."

"What?"

Rather than answer right away, Deegan finished eating his chocolate as if nothing else mattered. As if it wasn't the wee hours of the morning. As if I weren't the type of person contemplating hurling this chair at his head. Well, scratch that last one; the chair was way too comfy to relinquish.

I settled for a stern glare. "Quit being cruel and tell me already. This isn't a suspense novel."

Seventeen

It was almost four in the morning when I finally closed the front door behind me and dropped my keys onto the table.

I'm not sure if I was more surprised to find my whole family awake, or that Jinx was included in the awake crowd. One look at the narrowed eyes and unmoving tail told me that I better greet my crotchety cat first and foremost.

"Good morning, Jinx." Scooping the fluffball into my arms, I collapsed onto the warm spot on the couch. "Did you miss me?"

"Mrrrow."

I petted him until the angry meow turned into a semblance of purring, starting and stopping if I slowed my attentions. When at last Jinx lay down and closed his eyes, I met the looks of curiosity and annoyance around the room. I was unsure if my mother was more annoyed that I'd stayed out all night or that I hadn't brought the detective home for breakfast. To be safe, I skipped her and spoke to the looks of curiosity instead.

"I staked out the graveyard tonight." To be honest, in hindsight, it wasn't my best lead-in but I blamed the lack of real sleep.

"You did what?" Mom spluttered.

Dad's forehead creased in a deep V. "Charity Basham, are you out of your mind?"

"You didn't invite me?" Grampy looked offended.

I let go of Jinx long enough to rub my tired eyes and received a knee full of claws in return as he stretched and jumped down. Gritting my teeth, I explained the rest of the evening in a rush.

"Don't worry, I wasn't by myself. Deegan showed up so I was perfectly safe. Plus, it turned out to be a kid named

Eric, Rex's teenage son, who was doing all of the digging, so he wasn't really a threat. Unless startled by a sneeze, but that's not the point." Seeing that the confused looks weren't clearing, I gathered my thoughts and tried to explain more coherently.

"Eric recently moved here with his dad and doesn't have any friends yet. On top of that, Deegan said that Eric felt even more alone because of all the time his dad had been spending with Kira." I didn't think Kira was all that much older than Eric, but that was neither here nor there. "Anyway. Eric's been playing these geocaching games on his phone."

"Geo-who?" Grampy interrupted. He wiggled a finger in his ear as if to clear it.

"Geocaching," I repeated slowly. "It's like hide and seek with boxes of stuff instead of people. And there's not really a time limit. You can use GPS or other ways to navigate to the hiding spot, dig up the cache, and leave something behind if you take something out so that others can also play and find it later."

"It's become quite popular," Dad added, surprising me. I guessed geocaching must have caught on in Florida, too.

"Well, as it happens, Eric's particular geocache challenge this past week was to solve a math equation and use the answers as part of coordinates. He solved the problem wrong several times, inputting the wrong longitude and latitude into his GPS app because of it. He admitted that after the first two tries, he just started digging in the hopes of finding the cache without the coordinates."

"Well, I'll be." Grampy said. "Just goes to show kids need to be paying more attention in school, now doesn't it." He closed his recliner.

"Wait. You didn't hear the rest." I didn't wait quite as long as Deegan had when he told me, but I did pause for effect. "Instead of pressing charges, Brother Joseph agreed with Deegan's recommendation to enroll Eric in group math tutoring instead."

Mom clapped her hands. "A kind of 'punishment to fit the crime' scenario. Great idea. Maybe the young man will learn something after all."

"And he might even make some friends," Grampy said. "Now, who wants breakfast?"

***

"See, I knew you could figure it out." Margo said.

We were all clustered around a winter wonderland display in Sassy Supplies. Although I'd decided to keep the store closed today after my whirlwind night, I still had plenty to do to get the place ready for all of the after-Christmas discount sales. Margo and Rita had agreed to meet me after lunch to help. While we worked, I gave them the full scoop about the guilty party in the grave diggings.

"I don't know that I'd say I figured it out. More like I was in the right place at the right time." It pained me to admit, but I had to tell them that Deegan would have caught Eric even without me.

"How is the Dishy Detective, anyway?"

"Not you, too!" I expected such comments from Margo, but from quiet Rita it was a complete shock.

"Hey, it's catchy." She smiled, a small twinkle in her eye.

I smoothed a few hairs that had come loose from my headband, not having the energy to scold either sister. It was nice to see Rita's spirits rising. Ever since the events of Halloween, she'd been a little down. Besides, they weren't wrong; Deegan was nice to look at.

"He's doing alright." I finally answered, taping the last side of a fifty-percent-off sign into place above a rack of glittery snowflakes. "The stubborn man wouldn't see a doctor right away but thankfully when he did get checked out this morning there was no concussion. He said he had a headache that would make a jackhammer seem tame, though, and went home to sleep."

My heart still stuttered a little when I thought how bad that hit from the shovel could have been. I still felt a little guilty, too, truth be told. Even though I told Margo and Rita that Deegan would have caught Eric eventually, part of me was pretty sure he wouldn't have spent Christmas evening in a graveyard if he hadn't been looking out for me.

"Hello, earth to Charity!" Margo snapped her fingers in front of my face.

"Sorry. Did you say something?"

She pointed. "Your sign is upside down."

"Maybe you should go take a nap, too." Rita patted my back.

"Maybe you're right." I sighed.

"Well, we'll get out of your hair."

Margo's heels clicked all the way to the door. "Later, girl. Don't you forget to call us when you start your next mystery."

"Next mystery?" I stuck my finger with a thumb-tac and winced. "I don't plan to have a next mystery."

"You never do," she winked.

Hearts

&

Hostages

Katherine H. Brown

Hearts & Hostages

One

"These pillows were such a beautiful idea, Dana." On impulse, I gave the older woman a hug. "And the fact that we get to give them to breast cancer patients at the hospital makes each one even sweeter."

Dana straightened the hem of her sweater. "Do you think so?"

"Look around." I waved a hand at the tables packed with people. The sound of whirring sewing machines almost overpowered all other noises. In another corner, a small group of ladies sat stuffing heart-shaped pillows with fluffy polyester filling. I smiled widely. "I didn't think we could top last month but this is by far the largest group we've had for craft night. If you keep bringing in ideas that draw this many crafters at a time, we'll have to host two classes instead of one just to have enough seating!"

It was the truth. I may have hired Dana Stieger on accident, actually she kind of misinterpreted something I said and hired herself, but there was no denying the boom in business since she had taken over craft nights at my store, Sassy Supplies Crafts & More. For a Thursday evening, the place was really hopping.

"Everyone loves to help a good cause," Dana said modestly, tucking her chin down. "We have a town full of generous people, that's all. Speaking of generous, thank you for donating all of the thread and filling to the project. It made it so much simpler for people to purchase fabric alone and have everything else available here."

"My pleasure." I tossed my long, light, light, light, light brown hair—some people mistakenly call it blonde—over my shoulder and continued making my rounds.

It was fun greeting customers and providing tips or assistance where I could. A few ripped seams, a hunt for extra stuffing, and before we knew it craft night was wrapping up.

"Excellent job everyone!" Dana clapped her hands. "If you have any unfinished heart pillows, please leave them on the front table. Charity and I will get them stuffed and closed up in time to deliver to the hospital tomorrow."

I nodded. "That's right. And before you leave, I wanted to give you the current total of finished pillows. Drum roll please!" Becca, my cashier and overall store assistant, rapped out a beat on her legs on cue. "As of my count five minutes ago, we have a total of two-hundred twelve completed pillows! That is a lot of pillows to gift a lot of hospital patients."

Cheers and whoops of excitement resounded, none louder than Margo. But then, I couldn't remember a single person ever being louder than Margo. At anything. She was the exact opposite of her reserved twin sister Rita, in both personality and wardrobe.

***

Friday morning, Becca covered the customer end of things while I hand-stitched a small stack of pillows closed. There were pillows in every shade and pattern from hot pinks to soft yellows, swirls, stripes, florals; you name it, there was a pillow from it. My favorite pillow was made of a midnight blue fabric with a shimmery, silver moon and stars pattern.

I absolutely couldn't wait to see the look on the faces of the many women we would be gifting with the pillows.

"Becca, I'm running these out to the car." I closed the box on the last bunch and headed out the front of the shop where I'd parked today.

Lola opened the door for me. "I'm on my way out, let me help."

"Thanks." Lola Richards was a sweetheart. She'd moved to town just before Thanksgiving and we'd become friends pretty quickly.

After I ruled her out as a murder suspect.

But that's a story for a different day.

No sooner had I opened the rear of my white SUV then my cell phone rang. I juggled the box over to one hip but nearly dropped it as I tried to reach for the phone in my pocket with my other hand.

"Here, let me."

Happily, I passed the box off to Lola, answering the phone just before the ringing stopped. "Hello?" I closed the car and locked it after Lola loaded the box in with the other two. On the phone, Dana Stieger was practically shouting. "Dana, slow down, please. I'm having trouble understanding you. Is everyone okay? Okay. Okay, yes." I nodded, though I knew Dana couldn't see me. "It's not a problem. I can take the pillows or find someone to help me. Thanks for letting me know."

"Didn't mean to eavesdrop, but is Dana alright?"

"Yes. There is some kind of problem with the car. First, I was afraid they'd been in an accident but she said it just won't start. Bill is trying to figure out what's wrong. She was distraught about not being able to help deliver the pillows she finished." I leaned against my own car, thinking. "If I left now, I might be able to grab them and make it back only a little late for the drop-off appointment today at the hospital."

"Why don't you let me run get the pillows and meet you at the hospital?" Lola offered. "Then you won't have to run off from work early and you can still be on time.”

“Are you sure?”

“Positive.” She nodded firmly her bright red hair swinging about her shoulders. “I’m not busy at all and I’d love to help pass out the pillows.”

“Perfect!”

The next half hour flew by as I worked with Becca. With Valentine’s Day this Saturday, we had a rush of customers coming to get materials for handmade gifts.

The bell jingled again and I smiled widely at Margo and Rita as they entered. “Hello, ladies! What brings you by today?”

“You know,” Margo put a hand on her hip. “I just got to thinking, I’d really like to go help deliver those pillows. Could you and Dana use another hand?" Dressed in a black leather jacket and red pantsuit, she looked more ready for a date than a trip to the hospital.

"Funny you should ask." I filled her in on the situation with Dana's car. "Lola went to pick up Dana's boxes of pillows, but I'm definitely not one to turn down help. Rita, did you want to come, too?"

"Umm. I could sit in the car, I guess." She tugged at the collar of her blush pink blouse, looking down. Total opposites, those sisters. "I'm not a big fan of hospitals. They make me really nervous."

I hated the idea of Rita stuck hanging out in the parking lot by herself.

An idea came to me as another string of customers came in, this time two adults and a group of kids. "I have another way you could help without going to the hospital."

"Really?" Rita looked up at me, worry lines melting away from her eyes. "What is that?"

"Do you think you could stay here and help Becca with anything? It might just be bagging items, or tidying aisles when people don't put things back in the proper places."

"Oh, that would be fine by me!"

Rita clapped like she'd just dodged jury duty or won the lottery and I nearly laughed out loud. "It's settled then." I turned to Becca. "Put Rita to work and I'll be back in time to help you close the store."

Two

"Good morning." Wynona, long-time receptionist for Becksville General Hospital, greeted me and Margo in monotone voice that precisely matched the tired expression on her face.

The woman was a fixture. I remembered her being here every single day that I came to visit my Grandma Alice before she passed. Today, she looked more like she should be lying down in a room rather than directing visitors to them. Straggling strands of gray hair stuck out from her head in all directions. Her lipstick, a muted burgundy, was smeared at one corner of her mouth, and no amount of makeup could conceal the dark circles beneath her eyes.

"Hi," I placed my two boxes on the floor and pulled a business card out of my pocket. Handing it across the counter, I pointed to the name. "I'm supposed to meet this gentleman today. He was going to take our group around the cancer ward to pass out some gifts for the breast cancer patients."

She handed the card back.

I waited as she answered two phone calls in rapid succession, immediately putting each on hold. No wonder her forced smile didn't meet her eyes. From what I could hear, the people shouting on the other end of the phone were unhappy over something.

"Fifth floor," she said abruptly. Her hand hovered over the phone. "Elevator's broken so you'll have to take the stairs. Mr. Leach is the second office on the left." With a flick of her wrist, she pointed the direction I needed to go.

"Thanks." It was no use. Wynona was already back on the phone and trying to calm someone down. I sent a text to Lola with instructions to come to the fifth floor, then hoisted my boxes and turned to Margo. "I guess we go that way."

Thank goodness the boxes of fluffy pillows weighed almost nothing. That, plus all of the Krav Maga I'd been doing lately for exercise might just be the only reason I made it up five flights of stairs without getting winded. Margo worried me, teetering in four-inch heels as she was. My fears were unfounded. She kept up and nearly passed me when we reached the last landing.

I looked at her shoes before heading down the hall. "How in the world did you manage five flights without toppling over in those stilts?"

"These are one of my shorter pairs," she laughed. "And to answer your question,

Stairmaster. Every day. I could climb stairs in my sleep."

At the second door on the left, I paused. "Here's Mr. Leach's office." The letters on the door simply read HR Coordinator. Hand poised to knock, I stopped as loud yells came from inside. The noise quieted. I waited another few seconds then took a deep breath.

Knock-knock.

The door opened. A balding man with wire-frame glasses opened the door. His glasses lenses were so thick, they mimicked magnifying glasses and made his eyes look unsettlingly owlish.

"Mr. Leach?" I peered over his shoulder. The man's serene smile seemed so at odds with the previous sound of yelling, I was shocked to see he was alone in the office when I peered.

"Yes?"

"I'm Charity Basham and this is Margo." While not heavy, the boxes were starting to get cumbersome. I definitely couldn't offer to shake hands. Shifting, I nodded at my load. "We brought the heart pillows for the patients. Dana couldn't make it this morning but said you were the person who would be taking us around?"

"Quite so. You are two minutes late."

He spoke without dropping the odd smile, so I wasn't sure if it was a complaint or simply an observation. I inclined my head in acknowledgement. "Yes, I know. I'm so sorry. The elevators were down."

Mr. Leach stepped into the hall so quickly that I nearly dropped the top box trying to scoot out of his way. "Let's get going, shall we?"

"Charity!"

"Hey, Lola." I turned as my friend called out from behind us. "You're just in time."

Burdened with two boxes of her own, Lola tossed her head, trying and failing to remove several strands of red hair from across her eyes.

"Ladies." Mr. Leach took off at a brisk walk leaving us no choice but to follow right away.

So much for resting my arms a second. By the time we'd wound around multiple hallways and one more set of stairs, going down this time, I had come to a new conclusion about pillows. They evidently gain weight over time.

"Here we are." Mr. Leach scanned a badge to open a door. It led us into a wing that spread out in an octagon shape, hallways branching every which way. He checked his watch, something I'd noticed him doing frequently during our walk here. "Eight hallways, six patients down each hall, check in at the nurse's station before you start so you don't get kicked out."

"Oh." Taking a moment to set down my boxes and stretch my back, I sidestepped in front of Mr. Leach. "Dana spoke as if you would be taking us from room to room. At the very least, wouldn't you vouch for us with the nurses so they know it is okay for us to be roaming around?"

I hadn't visited many hospitals lately, but I knew things were supposedly stricter than they were a few years ago. So far, I wasn't seeing any evidence of it.

It seemed odd that we didn't get visitor badges or introductions of some kind.

As, Mr. Leach looked at the time once again, I asked, "Do you have another meeting?"

"No. Nowhere." Mr. Leach said, his glance at his watch belying his words.

"I'm sure introducing us to the nurses won't take more than a moment. If you don't have time to walk with us to the patients after that, we completely understand." This wasn't going at all how Dana had led me to expect.

I counted at least three blinks of those giant eyes before he said, "Of course."

The way he managed to sound so annoyed yet keep that peaceful smile fixed in place started to give me the creeps. I glanced at Lola. She shrugged and we joined him at the large rectangular nurse's station.

Two female and one male nurse sat behind the high desk. Only one of the women looked up.

"These ladies are here to pass out pillows. Give them a quick hand, will you?" With a wave and a nod, Mr. Leach turned to leave.

Then all of the lights went out.

Three

Well, not all of the lights.

Red flashing lights blazed to life in the darkness. Slowly, an electrical hum pulsed through the room and the computers flickered back to life, casting an eerie glow to the faces of the three nurses in the dim wing.

"What in the world?" Margo yelped.

Someone bumped me. I dropped both boxes on my foot as Mr. Leach fumbled past.

"No, no, no." His grumbling didn't cover the sound of him yanking on the door. Nor the thud as he hit or kicked it when it refused to open.

"What's going on?" I asked the room at large. "Some kind of drill?"

The three nurses at the desk scrambled to patient rooms without answering. I watched in the bizarre red lighting as they entered room after room, heard them assuring everyone that things were fine. Shortly, the last one disappeared around a corner.

Mr. Leach remained by the door.

Wanting answers and with limited options, I decided to see what he knew. As I walked up to him, I could see the small glow from a cell phone. Only whispered words from his conversation floated to my ears.

Not ready. Stick to it. No more.

The fragments made no sense. "Mr. Leach? Do you know what's going on with the lights?"

The moment I spoke, he turned those giant eyes on me. Creepier than ever with red light reflected in his lenses, they blinked rapidly. "No. Not at all. I'm sure everything will be right as rain. We have generators, you know."

Generators. That explained why the computers and, I assumed, patient machines had come back online. "Oh. Okay. What about the door?"

Smile not wavering at all, Mr. Leach shook his head. "Stuck tight, I'm afraid."

"Alrighty, then." I backed away.

"Well, what'd he say?" Margo was leaning against the nurse's station, arms crossed. Lola stood beside her, curling a strand of hair around her finger. Funnily enough, it looked less red now that the wing was blinking out red lights all over the place.

I rubbed my temples, dreading the headache I could feel starting from the strobe-light effect the emergency red flashers were giving off. "He said the door is stuck and that's about it."

Lola dropped her hand from her hair. "What do we do now?"

I worried my bottom lip with my teeth for a second. The nurses weren't back yet. I shrugged. "We came to deliver pillows. I say, let's go deliver some pillows. The patients could probably stand to have a distraction. I know I could."

"Okay, let's go." Lola pulled out her keyring and used one key to cut through the tape on her box. "Stay together or split up?"

"Let's stay together for this first hall and then we can split when it branches out." I looked down at the boxes on the floor. "Maybe we can just carry two and stash the others here behind the nurses' desk. I'd hate for someone to trip over them in the dark.

Margo and Lola agreed.

"Charity, this one has a hole in it."

I leaned around Margo. "A pillow?"

"No. The actual box." She pointed to one of the two I'd brought.

Sure enough, one entire corner was missing. "It's a good thing there were only pillows inside. Something smaller would have fallen out." As I spoke, the white fur pillow inside shifted. I narrowed my eyes. "Did anyone see fur being used when we had craft night?"

"Fur?" Lola crinkled her brows.

"Mm-hmm. Like, faux white fur."

"Nope."

I turned to Margo. She also shook her head in the negative. Closing my eyes, I willed the fur to have been my imagination before turning back to the box.

It was still there.

Tentatively, I reached in one hand.

"Ow!" I jerked my hand back as tiny teeth nipped it. "Jinx. Get your furry tail out of that box," I hissed. "You are in big trouble, Mister."

A white paw whipped out the hole and disappeared back inside. Obviously, someone was in a mood.

Sigh. I borrowed Lola's key and opened the top of the box. My pensive

Persian cat peered up at me. "These are not your pillows," I told him.

Jinx stared. My cat was a cat of only a few talents. One of them was the unblinking stare.

I plucked Jinx unceremoniously from the box. "We have a stowaway."

"Oh my gosh!" Lola covered a laugh.

Margo peeked inside the box. "Did anyone bring a lint roller?"

***

With Lola carrying the two boxes, Margo's arms loaded with pillows—mostly devoid of cat hair after much brushing and patting—I led the way to the first room. Jinx squirmed in my arms but I held tight.

"Hi," I popped my head around the jamb of the open door.

Creaking sounded as the patient moved around. "Are you here to fix the lights?"

"No, my friends and I are just visiting. We brought gifts." I held up a pillow, though she probably couldn't tell what it was from so far away. "May we come in?"

"Sure."

It was a relief to step into the room where there were no bright red lights blinking incessantly. The glow and hum of machines provided an odd ambiance. I gave my eyes a second to adjust, then moved closer to the bed. Margo and Lola trailed behind.

"I'm Charity. These are my friends Margo and Lola." Running a hand down Jinx's fluffy coat to elicit a purr, I nodded to him, as well. "And this fellow is Jinx. For today, he believes he's a therapy cat."

As if in agreement, Jinx used my distraction to jump onto the bad. I made a grab for him but the lady only laughed. "Hello to you, too." She scratched behind Jinx's ears, a sure-fire way to make a friend for life. "My name is Nadia. I left my three fur-babies at home. Please, don't worry about Jinx. It's nice to have someone to pet."

We talked with Nadia for four or five minutes. The whole time, I hoped power would be restored. When we left the room, nothing had changed. Well, one thing had: Mr. Leach had disappeared. Unfortunately, the darkness and flashing red lights were the same.

Just for kicks, I tried the door before we ventured farther into the ward.

Still locked tight.

We visited two more rooms before reaching the end of the first hall.

"Okay. Let's split up."

Margo held up a hand to stop me. "You can't go by yourself. Carrying Jinx, a box of pillows, and passing them out, not to mention possibly having to open doors," she gestured at two closed doors down the hall to our right. "You're talented, but even you only have two hands."

"It's fine. I'll go by myself this way." Lola inclined her head left. "Margo, you help Charity. We'll surely all meet back at the nurses' station around the same time."

"Okay, if you're sure." Jinx twitched his tail so that it hit me square in the nose and mouth. "Pfft. We're going, we're going."

The next woman Margo and I visited was sleeping. Leaving the pillow on her bed, we tiptoed back out. Four more grateful women later and our hallway was finished.

"Only four more rooms on this hall," Margo said. "This room is marked *Supply Closet*."

As I followed her past the closet door, Jinx squirmed and wriggled. When I tightened my grip, the cranky cat clawed me. "Ouch!" It was such a surprise that I lost my grip and let him jump free.

Jinx ran back to the closet door and yowled.

"Shhh. This is a hospital. You can't make so much racket." My effort to scoop him up was met with a hiss.

"What's going on?" Margo backtracked, looking from me to my frazzled feline.

"No idea." I knelt down in front of Jinx. "He's never acted like this. Even when he was mad at me for forgetting to feed him. Attitude, yes, but actually scratching and clawing aren't normal."

"Maybe there's some catnip or something in that closet."

My eyes narrowed on a rust-colored spot beside Jinx's paw. Roughly the size of a penny, it was shimmery and wet. Jinx stepped away from the door and a larger spot was visible behind him. And on the edge of the doorframe....

"Oh my gosh!" This time, satisfied that I was paying attention, Jinx let me pick him up again. "Margo. Do you see that?"

Four fingerprints were just visible across the door jamb, below the handle.

Four smeared, blood-red fingerprints.

Four

"Well, don't just stand there!"

Margo's yell made me jump. "What do you suggest we do?" I stepped forward.

"Not whatever it is you're currently thinking of doing," she answered.

I took another step, reaching out my hand.

"Especially if you're thinking of opening that door."

Ignoring her, and all of the self-preservation instincts screaming inside of me, I turned the knob.

My stomach flipped. "Call 911," I said. I tried to position myself in front of the door.

"911? We're in a bloody hospital! Emphasis on the word bloody." Margo's heels clicked as she stepped over and leaned around me. "Oh, dear!"

Oh, dear didn't cover the half of it. Scrunched inside the closet was one of the three nurses we had seen briefly. This one, a tall, muscular woman, had a large gash over her left eye.

Jinx jumped down again, this time away from the closet. I was too focused on breathing to go after him.

"Is she…you know…dead?" Margo's voice had dropped to a normal, indoor discussion level. For Margo, that was practically whispering.

"How should I know?" I asked.

She gave me a pointed shove. "You've done this kind of thing before. Go check and see."

"There's usually less blood," I grumbled. She had a point though. Loathe as I was to admit it, being squeamish around a body didn't really make sense at this point.

I reached for her wrist.

A bloodcurdling scream sounded and I nearly fell right on top of the poor woman.

The scream hadn't been from her.

Nope. Based on the lack of pulse, she was dead.

The scream had come from somewhere down the hall. The screaming ceased. The yells that took its place were even more chilling. "Charity! Margo!"

Margo and I turned to each other with wide eyes. "Lola!"

Without a backward glance at the dead woman in the closet, I sprinted past Margo and down the hall.

And the next hall.

And the next.

Finally, I stopped. I couldn't run any more. Leaning against the wall, I clutched my aching side and drew in long slow breaths. So much for Krav Maga being good cardio.

There was no sign of Lola anywhere.

Jinx skittered up beside me. Margo caught up shortly after him.

"I didn't see her," I said. "But that doesn't mean anything. We haven't covered all of the halls yet. Maybe she found something awful, like we did."

Margo gripped my hand. "I found her box of pillows."

My stomach dropped to my toes.

"It was still in one of the patient rooms," Margo continued. "I noticed it when I stopped to take off my shoes." She held up a hand, the strappy leather heels dangling from a finger. "One of the straps broke. I guess maybe they don't make good running shoes, after all."

"Did you see any blood? Signs of a struggle?" I braced myself for the worst.

"No. Just the pillows."

I exhaled in relief. Maybe we just missed Lola or hadn't found her yet. "Maybe we should keep looking. If something spooked her, or she found something bad, she could be roaming around looking for us." I tried to convince myself as much as Margo. Thankfully, Margo didn't argue.

"We keep looking for her then." She glanced up and down the hall. "But I don't think we should split up."

"Nope, definitely not. We are sticking together." I looked down as Jinx sidled up to rub my ankles. "Yes, that means you, too, Mister." My hair fell across my face and I brushed it back as I stood. Then, after second thought, I pulled a ponytail holder off my wrist and pulled my hair into a messy bun. Having it out of my way seemed like a good idea at this point. "Before we keep moving, we need to call the police."

Margo's phone rang at the same time that I reached for mine. "Rita," she said to me before answering. "Hello?"

Shouts could be heard through the phone pressed to Margo's ear. I paused. Rita shouting couldn't possibly mean anything good.

The conversation was a quick one. Margo hung up.

"Well? Don't leave me in suspense. What was all the yelling? Is the whole city having a blackout? Is the store okay?"

She placed her hands on her hips. "Yes, they're just fine. Rita was yelling at me about being caught up in a hospital that was being held hostage."

"Hostage?" I rubbed my head. It was safe to say my headache had ratcheted to migraine status about the time I found the body. "Oh crap! The body." I held up my index finger for Margo to wait, then scrolled to Deegan's name in my phone and hit send.

Voicemail.

"Call me!" I winced at how desperate that sounded, but these qualified as desperate circumstances. I nodded at my friend. "Go ahead and tell me about Rita. I'm going to text Detective Sota about the woman we found in the closet."

Deegan Sota had recently gotten back to Becksville after being gone the entire month of January. We had barely gotten off on the right foot, some light flirting rather than him threatening to arrest me all the time, when he'd been assigned the task of training at a month-long police academy somewhere in the northern part of the state. Once home, he'd been on double duty at work and I hadn't seen hide nor tail of him.

Needless to say, texting him about a dead body was not the first conversation that I'd imagined having with him once he was back in town.

As I typed out the message, Margo launched into her favorite pastime, storytelling. "Everything is fine at the store. All the lights are working. At least I assume so since Rita didn't say a thing about darkness, or closing early. No, she called to yell at me and tell me to get out of here. The power outage is no simple power outage according to Aunt Mildred, my momma's brother's wife. Nope. Aunt Mildred called Rita complaining about her shows not working because of some hostage computer monster taking over the hospital."

Amid trying to text and trying not to be frustrated at all of the extra details she felt the need to add, I had to admire her ability to not freak out or shut down in the midst of whatever chaos this was that we found ourselves in.

I hit send on my text, stuffed the phone in my back pocket, and grabbed Margo by the shoulders. "Slow down. None of that made sense. I've no idea who Aunt Mildred is—no, don't explain it again—but why would she know anything about the hospital anyway?"

"Oh. Well, she's here somewhere."

"Here?" I leaned closer. "Here, here? As in the hospital?"

"Here as in somewhere in the breast cancer ward." Margo waved her arms and I dropped my hands from her shoulders. "According to Rita, Aunt Mildred said in her call today that she didn't tell anyone that she had to have a double mastectomy because she was embarrassed. She was just going to tell people she'd gone on vacation if they looked for her. Then today, she overheard some yelling and arguing about hostages and computers and the lights went out. Well, she got scared and thought she better call somebody and tell them where she was at Before she could finish the conversation, Rita said the line went dead."

I tried to sort through all of that but my phone rang. "Deegan!" I answered. "Yes, I'm fine. Margo's with me. Yes, she's fine." The sound kept breaking up, punctuated by seconds of silence. I got the gist of what he was saying though. "Yes, the woman is dead. And we can't find Lola. No. No I haven't seen anyone being held hostage. The whole breast cancer ward is locked up tight, does that count? Hello? Hello?" The call cut out completely. I slipped my phone back in my pocket, frowning.

"Please tell me your knight in shining armor is coming to get us? Or, is he sending the police to get us, at least?" Margo clutched her high heels to her chest hopefully.

"No, the police can't do anything yet. People are trying to restore the power, though so far it isn't working." I picked up Jinx. "Back to plan A: let's try to find Lola.

After that, we need to find your aunt. Apparently, that hostage thing she called Rita about is for real."

Five

"Do you have a date for Valentine's Day this weekend?"

Margo's question stopped me in my tracks. "Seriously?"

She lifted her shoulders. "Hey, I'm always better with distraction. This seems like a situation in need of a distraction."

I lowered my voice to a whisper. "The situation where we're fumbling around in the dark hoping to find our missing friend, no more bodies, and possibly a clue as to what the heck is going on in this hospital? That situation?" We were on the last hallway before our circle brought us back up front to the nurses' station. I pointed to it, just visible around the corner in the flashing red lights. "This situation seems to me to require quiet and carefulness far more than distractions."

Margo attempted a lopsided grin. It turned into a grimace. "You're right. Sorry."

Guilt surfaced but I shoved it back down. Maybe I'd been a bit harsh. Maybe Margo was simply trying to conceal her own nerves. None of that mattered. What mattered was keeping ourselves off the radar of whatever violent person also lurked in these halls.

"Hey, we better turn our phones on silent," I whispered as the thought occurred to me. I'd seen one too many TV characters die due to untimely text messages. Not today!

"That's odd."

"What?" I asked.

"My phone had five bars when we got here. Now it has nothing."

A glance at my own screen showed the same. No bars, no service.

Great. One more problem that I can't solve.

I pocketed the now useless phone, took a deep breath, and quietly I led the way down the hall. We peeked in doors along the way. Each time I prayed to see Lola's face. Each time I grew more worried when she wasn't there.

Please, let Lola be okay! I prayed. *And us, too.*

"I'm going to go check the nurses' station. Maybe one of them is back." I handed Jinx to Margo. She handed me back one of her high heels. "What is this for?"

"Do you have any other weapons?" she raised an eyebrow.

"Ugh. Good point. Lord, I hope I don't need this shoe." I quieted my mumbling and tiptoed into the open space between our hall and the desk. I'd almost reached it when something furry brushed my ankles. I stifled the scream bubbling up from my throat and nearly punched Jinx before I realized it was only my cat and not a killer. I looked back at Margo who shrugged helplessly from her crouched position in the wall. She made a clawing motion and glared at Jinx.

Resigned to my fearless feline leading the way, I crept to the desk. Since I was coming up from behind it, I noticed the empty chairs first. The pair of legs sprawled on the floor didn't come into sight until I was nearer. Closing my eyes, I counted to three, hefted the shoe over my head, then inched behind the desk.

My eyes searched the scene. I exhaled a breath I didn't know I'd been holding. There was no blood. Also, the male nurse sprawled on the floor was tied, hands and feet, with what appeared to be hospital socks. If he was tied up, it stood to reason he was also alive. Jinx sniffed the prone man, then jumped into one of the chairs to sit.

I turned and motioned for Margo to join me.

"Not good."

"Nope." I pressed my face into my hands. *Think. Think. Think.* Another look at my cell confirmed we still had no service. I took a picture of the man and sent it to Deegan anyway, hoping that whenever a signal popped up the picture would send automatically.

"Do we untie him?"

Margo's continued attempts to whisper, while still louder than most people, was a sure sign of the gravity of the situation. And possibly an indication that I was good at being bossy, when needed. "Let's wake him up first." The thought of him waking up while we were loosening his bonds, possibly him being confused and trying to fight us off, well, better safe than sorry.

"How should we wake him?"

Before I could answer Margo, Jinx pounced right onto the man's stomach.

"Ugh!"

I grabbed Jinx and laid a hand on the guy's arm. "Shh. It's okay. We aren't going to hurt you." Based on his darting eyes and scowl, I didn't think he believed me yet.

"Tell that to my stomach," he muttered. "What did you do, drop a bowling ball on me?"

Jinx swiped a paw. The man moved his body just fast enough to escape a scratch on the shoulder. "Careful. Jinx is a little sensitive about his weight." I rocked back on my heels. "Listen, we found you tied up and we also found another of your coworkers in a supply closet." I couldn't bring myself to tell him she was dead.

Margo chimed in. "We don't know what the heck is going on. We were hoping you could tell us who tied you up pretty as a package. You know, so we could avoid them at all costs."

"I didn't see anything." He shifted, rocking back and forth until he came into a sitting position. "Can you untie me, please?" He continued talking as I moved behind him to work his wrists free from the long, tan sock. "

The nurse, Benjamin according to his name badge, rubbed his wrists. "I had just come back up front. I was leaning over the computers to reach the phone when something slammed into my head." He reached behind one ear. "I don't know what they hit me with, but this goose egg is pretty gnarly." Benjamin untied his own feet.

I couldn't help but be grateful it wasn't worse than a bump. Even a possible concussion was better than a bashed in skull.

"Who did you say was in the closet?"

"Umm. She was larger, and tall. Really dark brown hair." Thankfully, that description worked because my brain couldn't yet sort out what I'd seen enough to give further details.

"It sounds like Cheryl."

"Do you think the other nurse, the itty bitty one who was on shift with you when we came in could have done that?" Margo pointed at Benjamin's head.

"No way." He shook his head and winced. Moving with more care, he said, "That would be Zuri. She wouldn't hurt a fly. Literally. She couldn't even step on a spider last week. Broke down crying when I killed it in front of her." He swayed when he tried to stand. "Plus, no offense to Zuri, I don't think she is big enough to swing anything with enough force to cause a knot this size."

I let Benjamin's statement stand. He knew Zuri and I didn't. Her petite stature and quiet manner when we had been introduced this morning led me to believe him. For now, we'd assume she was also missing instead. Two people missing made me twice as nervous. "Okay, so we need to find our friend, Lola, and your coworker, Zuri. And we need to do it quickly and quietly," I added.

"What about Cheryl? Is she on her way or is she looking for Zuri?"

I glanced at Margo who nodded. "Cheryl is dead."

Benjamin looked back and forth between us. "Dead?"

I filled Benjamin in with as few details as possible. "No pulse. No responsiveness," I reiterated. Still, he insisted on checking.

"You're not a nurse. Maybe you missed something," he said as he rushed away.

There wasn't anything I could do to stop him. I hated splitting up, but in the end, Margo and I knew our priority was Lola. Because we'd continued forward when searching for her, we hadn't been back to the first to hallways yet. "Keep an eye out for anything that seems weird." Margo didn't ask me what qualified as weird and I was glad since I really had no clue. It seemed like something that needed to be said though.

Jinx padded down the hallway. I'd given up on holding him. If he was insistent on going first, it seemed like a good idea to me. People touted the abilities of animals in crisis situations and I knew Jinx to be intelligent. If my fearless feline had a sixth sense for danger, all the better for us.

I did snag a stapler and a pyramid shaped paperweight off of the desk, for good measure. They were heavier than the shoe. It irked me that there were no scissors to be found, but work with what you have, right? Margo followed my lead. She grabbed a clipboard with one hand, kept a red heel gripped in the other, and nodded that she was ready to move.

As we tiptoed forward, I listened closely for more screams, the sounds of doors opening and closing, footsteps, anything. Silence met my ears. I glared up at the ceiling; my headache pulsed with each flashing red light.

The first room looked exactly as it had when we dropped off the pillow earlier, though Nadia was asleep now, so I kept walking. The second room was strangely empty. It gave me pause. Out of curiosity, I whispered for Jinx and stepped inside. The sheets were thrown back as if the patient had recently gotten up. Only a thick slice of darkness was visible beneath the bathroom door, so I assumed she wasn't in there.

"Hello?" Margo whispered from just inside the door.

I heard the slightest noise from behind the bed.

"It's Charity and Margo," I called softly. "We're just here to check on you and ask if you've seen our friend, Lola."

Seconds ticked by as we waited. It didn't seem anyone would answer.

Finally, the patient lifted her head above the bed. Assured, she stood all the way up, pushing aside cords and lines hooked form her to the machine behind her.

"Here, let me help you." I rushed over to hold the cords out of the way. Margo fluffed the pillows and pulled the blankets up. When we had her settled comfortably, I noticed how young she looked up closely. Probably my age, thirty at best. I couldn't imagine being in her position.

"I'm Kelly. You said you were looking for your friend?" she asked.

I nodded. "The red-haired woman who was with us earlier today. We can't find her. Have you seen her again?"

"No, I'm sorry." Kelly fiddled with the sheets on her stomach, her eyes not meeting mine.

Following my suspicion, I stepped closer to ask my next question. "But you saw something, didn't you? Something that made you hide behind your bed?"

Margo, who had alternately been listening to us and poking her head out the door to keep an eye on things, scooted closer to me and Kelly's bedside.

"Please."

Kelly's fingers gripped the sheets tighter. I waited. At last, she gave a tiny nod. "I saw somebody get hit over the head." She gave a shudder. "I didn't see who did it. I was getting thirsty but I couldn't find the call button on the bed with the lights out. The dark makes me nervous so I'm sure I just missed it on the side of the bed."

I felt sorry for the bed sheets as Kelly continued nervously scrunching and rolling them.

"I was going to call out," she said. "To one of the nurses. I've got a view of the desk but only the half on this side of the hallway. As I opened my mouth to call out, a large hand came down with the desk phone, slamming it into the back of Nurse Benjamin's head." Kelly swallowed convulsively.

Margo slipped into the bathroom and returned with a small paper cup of water. "Here, drink this."

"Thank you." Kelly drained the cup. "Whoever hit him, they left down the other hallway. I never saw them."

Jinx wound between my ankles and I picked him up.

Margo refilled Kelly's cup once more and we continued our slow search for Lola.

In the hallway where we'd found the body, I saw a familiar figure.

"Benjamin?" I looked at the nurse, his head bowed into his knees as he sat sentry outside of the supply closet door. He'd draped a clean sheet over Cheryl's body.

"Why?"

I shook my head. "I have no idea. I'm so sorry for your loss."

We stayed there in silence for several minutes. At length, Benjamin gathered himself and stood. "You didn't find your friend yet?" he asked, though the answer was apparent.

"No." Margo sighed.

"Benjamin, is there anywhere that someone could be keeping her? And maybe nurse Zuri or any other hostages? A large break room? An office? Cafeteria in this wing that we might have missed? Unless he finally managed to open the door, Mr. Leach is also unaccounted for."

"Hostages?"

"We think so."

Margo nodded. "My aunt overheard a conversation. We haven't been able to ask her about it personally yet. Oh! You probably know where her room is. Can you take us to see Mildred Duvall?"

"Mildred. Hmm." Benjamin rubbed his neck. "Older lady? Talks a lot? Possibly talks more than she actually breathes?"

I snorted. Sounded like someone I knew. Rubbing Jinx behind the ears, I pretended my amusement was at the cat cuddled in my arms.

Margo smiled widely. "You nailed it. Where's her room?"

Dragging himself up the wall to a stand, he looked at the sheet-draped form one last time then closed and locked the door. "This way. I'll take you."

Six

"Auntie M!"

The yell made me jump. So much for that talking quietly skill she'd been practicing. Margo was back at full volume the moment Benjamin led us into Mildred Duvall's hospital room.

"Margo, is that you?" The older lady groped around the bedside table until her hand landed upon a pair of hot pink glasses. "Where's Rita?"

"She's not here."

"What?" Mildred shrieked. "You two never go anywhere alone."

I turned around and closed the door to the room. I doubted it muffled the noise much but if we could avoid alerting the entire floor to our whereabouts, that'd be great with me.

Margo's explanation about Rita and hospitals giving her the heebie jeebies floated to my ears as I kept watch through the windows. Benjamin paced back and forth, rubbing the knot on his head occasionally.

When the conversation swerved toward more members of their family, I decided it was time to steer Margo and her aunt back on track.

"Speaking of Rita, she told us you believed you overheard some type of conversation about hostages and, what was it, computers?" I left my post at the windows and joined Margo at the bedside. Even Benjamin snapped out of his own personal problems and started paying attention.

Mildred looked pleased with the opportunity to tell a story to a crowd. She sat up taller, plumping her mound of pillows. And that's when I noticed one of them was neon pink and heart-shaped. With the darkness, it was hard to notice from the side of the room. Up close, I knew it had to be one of ours. "One minute." I tugged the pillow gently away from Mildred. Jinx took the opportunity to jump down and explore. "Where did you get this pillow?"

"A real sweetheart brought it in to me. I thought the pain meds were getting out of control because she strolled in here with hair as bright as the Little Mermaid. I asked her if she was lost, but she told me she came to deliver a gift." Mildred frowned. "You aren't taking it away, are you?"

Handing back the pillow, I told her about Lola. "That's why we're here. To find out anything you can remember about that conversation or the people having it." I reached out, grasping Mildred's wrinkled hand. "Please, tell us as much as possible but maybe keep it quiet, just in case."

Mildred rubbed her hands up and down the neon pink pillow. "Let's see. It was not too long after your friend Lola dropped this off that I heard raised voices." She nodded. At least two. They were having an argument of some kind and at first, I didn't pay very much attention. You see, Agnes in the room across the hall is a yeller. Benny here would know." A glance at Benjamin showed him nodding. Mildred continued, warming to her subject. "Agnes yelled about everything. The temperature, the television channels, the food, you name it. But Agnes punctuated the end of every sentence with a good many expletives, too. After a few minutes, I realized it couldn't be Agnes. Far too tame for her to be involved."

"Okay. So, it wasn't Agnes. Think. Did you recognize either of the two voices? Were they male? Female?" I hated being pushy but I couldn't help the feeling that we were running out of time. How long had Lola been missing now, an hour? Two? It wasn't like I'd checked my watch when we heard her scream. We'd been at the hospital for almost three hours. Wandering the halls in darkness, save the glaring red flashes of light, made it seem more like three days.

"Both people were female. One sounded familiar, but for the life of me I just can't place the voice." Mildred pursed her lips. Her head tilted as though she were listening again. "There was a slight echo, too. Like a microphone or a speaker."

"Thanks, Auntie M. Can you tell us what you remember them saying?" Margo asked.

"Of course. What, do you think I'm so old I've got the Alzheimer's?" She huffed. "Once I realized all the commotion wasn't just Agnes blowing a gasket about warm Jell-o, I listened a little closer. They didn't use any names but I got the feeling one of them was in charge. That one said make sure you keep the monster running so they don't get the computers up too fast. The second voice seemed frustrated. She was also the one who echoed. Said that she was trying but that she thought someone was coming in through the back door. The first woman said don't worry about it and that she had a whole ward of people to use as hostages for negotiating their terms."

"Terms?"

"I don't know. I couldn't hear much of anything after that. The voices got quieter then stopped altogether."

"Did you see anyone come or go down the hall?"

"Not a soul."

My shoulders slumped. It had been a long shot, but I'd been hoping so badly that we would learn something useful. A clue that sent us in the right direction. No clarity came, however.

We thanked Mildred for her time. Margo said her goodbyes as Benjamin and

I slipped into the hallway. "I don't know what to make of that," I said.

"Me neither."

"Poor Auntie M." Margo clucked her tongue as she joined us. "I hate the idea of leaving her all alone in there."

"It's okay if you want to stay."

"Are you sure?"

I could see Margo was torn. If it were my family, I'd want to be certain they were safe. "Yep. You go ahead. If Benjamin is up for it, we'll keep looking for Lola."

Margo, clipboard and heel in hand, wrapped me in a big hug. "Thanks, Charity. You be careful and go find our girl. I'll keep trying the phones."

The door shut behind Margo. Suddenly, I felt alone and exposed. "Jinx, Jinx!" My curmudgeonly cat halted several feet away, tossing me a look of aggravation. We engaged in a short standoff before he slowly came back to circle my legs again. Good. The last thing I needed was to lose my cat in this place, too.

"Hey," I turned to Benjamin. "Did you ever think of a place large enough to hold hostages?"

He tapped his chin then snapped his fingers as an idea lit up his face. "We do have a mall employee lounge."

"Let's go!"

As quietly as possible, I followed Benjamin down a hall and through a door designated for employees only. As we walked, I noted the doors we passed: equipment storage, restroom, linen closet. The employee lounge was at the end of the short corridor.

"I'll go first," Benjamin whispered.

"Wait!" I handed him my stapler. "Just in case," I shrugged.

Grabbing the door handle, I waited until he nodded then I jerked the door open and he sprang inside.

A high-pitched squeal sounded.

Seven

"Good grief, Ben. What are you trying to do, give me a heart attack?"

"Zuri?"

I assumed the conversation meant the employee lounge wasn't full of hostages after all. Stepping around the door, I nearly tripped over Jinx as my curious cat raced me inside. Automatically, I swiveled my head in both directions.

A sigh escaped. Relief coupled with disappointment. Only the petite nurse sat on a barstool, drinking a coffee.

Nobody else was in the room.

No Lola.

I massaged my neck. If we didn't find Lola soon, I felt like I was going to lose my mind. Benjamin began telling Zuri everything that was going on. Frustrated to have to live it once, I didn't want to stick around and hear about our predicament all over again. Remembering the other rooms that we had passed, I said, "I'm going to the restroom. Someone watch Jinx for me?"

Benjamin waved a thumbs up. I retraced our steps to the ladies' restroom.

And immediately wished I hadn't.

"Come in, come in."

Frozen, I stood half in and half out of the door gaping. Dim emergency lights blinked over the sink. Mr. Leach stood inside, the combination of dim lights and mirrors creating a spooky glow around him. Behind the still smiling Leach, I could just make out the color of Lola's hair on the other figure in the room. She was tied to one of the metal frames of a bathroom stall, arms raised in the air above her head.

"Run!" she yelled.

"Now, now." Leach grasped my wrist and dragged me inside. "That would be rude. You're already here after all." He whipped a bandana out of his pocket and started tying my hands behind my back.

The bandana-hand-tying was clearly a problem. I had to admit though, my headache appreciated the lack of blinking red lights. The door opened and my heart nearly burst in excitement as my mind placed the petite figure.

"Zuri!" I called to the nurse.

My excitement melted as she nudged the door open with a hip. "Get over here and help me, Leach. This guy is heavier than he looks."

After he finished with my hands, Leach pushed me against a stall near Lola and turned to help Zuri drag Benjamin into the room. An electrical chord, power strip still attached, bound his hands together.

"Seriously?" I couldn't help the shock. "I thought he was your friend."

Zuri scoffed. "This oaf? He has an ego the size of an MRI machine and the bedside manner of a zombie. It's nurses like him that prompt so many bad reviews for the hospital."

A static, crackling sound interrupted Zuri's diatribe. She pulled a walkie talkie from the waistband at the back of her scrubs. It sounded like police or emergency responders but before they said much, Leach snatched the walkie talkie.

"I'll take care of this. Watch them," he smiled his creepy smile at Zuri and rushed from the room.

"So, was it Mr. Leach who conked Benjamin over the head?"

"Stupid man. Why he left him lying there to wake up, I definitely don't understand." Zuri rolled her eyes.

My fingers found the knot in the bandana. A girl who liked to vent. Perfect. "If he's so stupid, why are you helping him?"

That struck a nerve. Zuri turned on me and I stilled my fumbling fingers.

"I'm not helping him," she sneered. "He's helping me. I'm just letting him think he's in charge. The old fool fancies himself in love with me. All it took was a few trips to his office in HR, complaining about the pay and treatment. Soon, we'll have a much better resource pull for pay and benefits."

"By holding us hostage?" Genuine confusion seeped into my voice, earning even more scorn.

"You two weren't even supposed to be here. Hang on. Weren't there three of you?" She waved a hand dismissively. "Anyway. We took the hospital hostage. The systems, the programs. Heck, even the lights. If the bosses that be want everything up and running again anytime soon, they'll give in to the changes we want made." Zuri smiled, a cold calculating smile that made me shiver. "Y'all are just added leverage if we need it."

Benjamin stirred and moaned.

I winced as Zuri kicked him in the head. He lay unmoving again.

I found myself wondering if she took a class that was a little more lethal than my own Krav Maga lessons. Then again, maybe she was just mean. It probably spoke volumes about my desperation to be in denial about our current circumstances that these were the meandering paths I found my thoughts on.

Zuri made certain my wandering thoughts were pulled back on track with her next statement. "Now, I hate to run but I've got to find that stupid cat. It tried to scratch me; can you believe it? Who brings a cat to a hospital anyway?"

"Wait!"

Zuri narrowed her eyes.

"You didn't tell us what your demands are. Or what is so bad about working here that made you do all of this in the first place.”

"Seriously?" Zuri rolled her eyes again. I began to worry they might stick that way. "You watch too many tired old movies. This isn't going to be the part where I blab and blab until someone comes to stop me.”

"What part is it then?" I asked. "The part where you realize you've made a horrendous mistake and untie us, vowing to make it all up by giving back to the community for the rest of your life?”

Lola, quiet this whole time, snickered. At least someone appreciated my humor.

"Puh-lease.”

Zuri clearly did not. She

"I, uh, I just wondered if you could untie me so I can go to the restroom?"

"Fat chance."

Zuri stalked out of the restroom and I sighed in relief. A few more seconds and I'd have the bandana off of my wrists. What was it with people and using bandanas for nefarious purposes? I shivered as I remembered Serena, the YouTube DIYer killed in my shop during the Thanksgiving holidays.

"Got it." With the last tug, I freed my hands. I dropped the bandana, thought better of it, and stuffed it into my pocket. Next, I worked at the knot on Lola's bandana. It had been tied much more securely than my own. By the time I loosened it, Benjamin was waking up again.

Lola rubbed the angry red marks on her wrists as Benjamin spluttered a string of profanities. "Where is that tiny little menace?" He growled. "I'll stuff her into a laundry chute for this."

It was hard to take his threats seriously, face down on the ground as he were. Still, the guy had been having a rough day.

"Here, let me help you." Lola rushed over and knelt beside Benjamin. She used her long purple fingernails to work furiously at the chord restraining him.

The seconds felt like half an hour.

I scurried to the door, cracking it open and squinting into the hallway. No sign of Zuri. Or Mr. Leach.

From behind me, I heard Lola introduce herself.

"Hey," I whisper-shouted. "What exactly are we going to do now? We need a plan before someone comes back."

"I don't know about you, but I'm not waiting around for anyone." Benjamin practically growled as he regained his feet. "I'm going to track down Leach and thank him for this knot on my head, and then Zuri for adding to it." His sway took a little umph out of his words.

"Here." Lola wrapped an arm around his waist. "Lean on me. You still look a little woozy."

"I feel a little woozy," Benjamin said as he stared at her.

"And I feel like I'm going to throw-up if you two don't cut out the puppy-dog eyes." Valentine's weekend or not, we plain didn't have time for it. "We have an escape to make, crazy people to avoid, and a cat to find."

Lola blushed and spluttered.

"What's your plan?" Benjamin asked.

I noticed he remained wrapped around Lola, leaning heavily on her, but at least he was focused.

"You know the hospital. Is there another exit from this wing that either won't be on lockdown or that we can bypass?"

He frowned. "I didn't even know the doors would lockdown just by some computer attack so 'fraid not."

That sucked but on to the next thing. "Any other landlines in the building since our cells aren't working? The phone at the front nurse's station, well, it's all busted up from being used to hit you over the head."

"Actually, yeah. There might still be one in the employee lounge since Zuri used the coffee maker when she bashed me in there."

"Okay. I'll check to see if the lounge is empty." I pointed my finger at them. "You two, see if you can't get Benjamin his balance back. If not, hide."

Slipping out of the restroom, I made my way quickly and quietly back to the employee lounge at the end of the hall. There was no window to peek through, so, I steeled myself and cracked the door open. Everything was quiet. No movement. The dim lights didn't afford an easy view but I took a chance and stepped inside. When nobody jumped out at me or bashed me over the head, I took it as a good sign.

I began my search for a phone methodically. First, I checked the table where the coffee machine would have been if Zuri hadn't used it as a bashing machine instead. Nothing. Next, I checked beside each piece of furniture on the walls and end tables. After a few stubbed toes on chair legs which I didn't see sticking out so far, I finally found the object of my search.

A large, black phone plugged in to the wall and sitting on a tiny table behind the couch; it was the most beautiful thing I'd seen all day.

Praying it worked, I lifted the receiver to my ear. At the sound of the dial tone, I nearly whooped with joy. My fingers were shaking so badly, I had to hang up and try again. I'd punched the third and last number when a voice made me jump and nearly drop the phone.

"Put it down," Zuri snapped.

I turned around to face her. When I didn't see Jinx anywhere, I wasn't sure if she'd found him or if my furry feline had escaped her wrath.

"I said, put it down." She picked up a small potted plant and tossed it at me.

The missile flew past me and busted against the wall. "Okay, okay! Please, don't hurt me, Zuri. I'm putting the phone down now." Slowly, I placed the phone back on the base. As I did, I stepped in front of it. Maybe Zuri wouldn't notice the phone didn't quite click into place.

"Now what, are you going to tie me up again, right here in the employee lounge of the breast cancer wing?" I held my hands up, praying somebody on the other end of the line could hear the conversation still. "And where did your partner, Mr. Leach go?"

"I told you. He's not my partner."

"Right, you're calling the shots. I remember now." I shrugged. "Sorry. So, does that mean you shut down the hospital with the cyber-attack?"

"No."

I watched Zuri cross her arms over her chest. A defensive posture, interesting. "So, that was his idea? He's the smart, techy guy and you're the pretty face playing on his emotions?"

If it were possible, her glare became even more fierce than when she'd been kicking Benjamin in the head earlier. As I thought of that, I hoped that he and Lola were somewhere safe.

"Enough questions from you." Zuri stepped away from the door, moving my direction. As if she'd sensed my thoughts, she asked, "Where did your buddies go? I assumed when the restroom was empty that I'd find you all together somewhere."

I sent up a silent prayer of thanks. At least wherever they were, Lola and Benjamin were safe. Maybe. Unless Leach had found them. I gave myself a mental slap. No negative thoughts needed, no ma'am. They were safe. I would believe it.

"Well?"

"No idea," I said honestly. "Last I heard, Benjamin was going to look for you. He had a special thank you to pass along."

"Ha! Good luck to him." Zuri stepped around a coffee table and I moved the opposite direction. She stepped back again, blocking the path to the door once more.

At least she hadn't launched any more décor at my head. I tried to keep her talking in the hopes that Benjamin and Lola would get me out of here soon. "You said you, or whoever actually orchestrated the cyber-attack, did it to get better working conditions?"

The open-ended question worked this time. Zuri nodded. "That's right. How would you like to work forty-eight or seventy-two hour shifts because not enough people show up? Or to have your holiday pay only cover eight hours regardless of the fact that you worked an entire holiday weekend? Patients yelling and cussing, throwing food; it isn't our fault the cafeteria sends up disgusting mush or that their doctor's send special diet instructions. No way do we get paid enough for harassment like we have to put up with in this place."

It was difficult for me to imagine any of the sweet ladies I'd met today acting that way, but pain and fear definitely brought out the worst in people so I supposed it was possible. "Even if you have a point, surely you could have spoken to your supervisors, petitioned the board, joined a union. Something!"

"Nobody would have listened." She shook her head. "No, this had to be done."

"And killing Cheryl? How did that help?"

Zuri blanched. For the first time, uncertainty replaced the looks of smugness and anger on her face. "What are you talking about?"

"Cheryl's dead. Her body stuffed in the supply closet. Did you hate her as much as you hate Benjamin?"

"You're lying."

"Afraid not. I saw her myself." I wouldn't be unseeing her for a long time, I felt certain, but didn't add that out loud.

Zuri's arms dropped to her sides. Her head dipped low. "No. I told Cheryl to get out. She wouldn't join me to make the hospital a better place, but I told her to leave so she wouldn't be caught in the middle. She was one of the only decent people here. A real work mom."

Movement caught my eye near the door. Zuri had left it ajar, barely. In my peripheral vision, I saw Jinx wriggle his way inside. I sucked in a breath and kept my gaze on Zuri, hoping she wouldn't notice my creeping cat as he stalked his way to me.

Before she even had the chance to see him, the door swung open behind Jinx.

"Deegan!" The shout left my mouth before I could stop it. Relief flooded me.

Zuri spun.

I braced myself but to my surprise, she didn't attack. She didn't even try to flee.

"Zuri Achianovi, you're under arrest."

I watched as Zuri meekly held out her arms. Then, she turned to me. "Make sure they find Leach. He has to pay for Cheryl."

Eight

I collapsed onto the couch, my legs wobblier than a bowl of Jell-o as Deegan handcuffed Zuri and read the Miranda Rights to her.

Jinx jumped up into my lap and sat, staring at me.

"Thanks for coming back for me," I said. I rubbed a hand along his back, his tail raising in pleasure as he purred.

"He did more than that," Deegan said.

"What do you mean?"

"Jinx strutted out from the side of the building. Next thing I know, he's shredding my ankles. I tried to pick him up but he ran off and then came back to claw me again. Finally, I followed him to an old laundry chute. It was too slick for him to climb up, but I got the impression he'd just come out of it. Up I went, and I'll be danged if your cat didn't attach himself to my calf and hitch a ride."

My eyebrows raised.

"That's not all," Deegan said. "He led me straight here to you. Of course, I could hear you talking the moment we entered the hall. He barreled straight ahead. Didn't want to share the hero spotlight, if you ask me."

I laughed out loud. It felt good, laughing. Way better than scared or holding my breath or on the verge of crying.

"Maybe instead of one hero, we should just say that you two make a good team." I smiled.

Deegan grinned. "Teams are fine with me, when they're the right ones." His wink nearly made my knees weak all over again.

"Oh my gosh!" I stood, scooping up Jinx along the way. "We have to find Lola and Benjamin. And check on Margo and her aunt. Plus find that looney Mr. Leach guy from HR."

"Slow down," Deegan grasped my arm as I tried to rush past him. "Let me get this one secure somewhere and then I'll help you look."

The lights suddenly flared to life. I'd never been so grateful for blinding white walls and shiny white floors as I was in that moment. It didn't feel cold and steril now; it felt bright and happy. Especially with the awful red blinking gone.

Deegan too looked relieved. "The team downstairs must have finally shut down the virus blocking the hospital's ability to come completely back online. That means a team of people are streaming up the stairs even as we speak. Leach will be caught in no time."

"Thank goodness!"

Zuri, still quiet, blinked in the bright lights.

"I think I know where you can stash her." I inclined my head toward the suddenly mute nurse.

Deegan followed me to the restroom and cuffed Zuri to a stall support pole. Only fitting in my opinion.

A scraping noise drew my attention to the back stall. "Lola?" I called. Maybe she and Benjamin had taken my advice to hide after all. At least, I hoped so. Otherwise, this bathroom had really big rodents from the sound of things.

"Charity?" came the whispered reply.

Dodging around Deegan as he tried to urge caution, I dashed to the last stall. Whipping open the door, I stared. Then started to chuckle again.

Lola, who had probably started out sitting on Benjamin's lap on the toilet tank, was squished against the wall with his upper half pinning her in place.

"He passed out again." She shifted, barely catching Ben from rolling off the toilet. "A little help please."

Deegan and I freed Lola from Benjamin's weight. She stood and stretched, rolling her neck and shoulders until her neck popped.

Deegan gently slapped Benjamin awake. "Can you keep him up until we can get a doctor or paramedic in here?" He asked Lola.

"Sure." She settled next to the male nurse, turned on a mega-watt smile, and said, "Hi. I'm Lola. My favorite color is red. Your turn."

It might be a bit unorthodox, but maybe playing twenty questions would keep Benjamin focused then. As he answered orange, I tapped Lola on the shoulder. "I'm going to find Margo. You sure you're okay?"

She waggled her eyebrows. "Oh, I'm perfectly happy right here."

Still laughing at Lola, I allowed Deegan to lead me into the hallway once more. Jinx wound around my ankles and I picked him up.

"Charity."

The serious look on Deegan's face halted my laughing. I assumed he was going to launch into lecture mode. Really, I couldn't blame him. The hospital power might be restored, but we were far from out of the woods yet. We still had to find Leach, and Margo, and be sure all of the patients were safe.

My rambling thoughts were interrupted as Deegan said, "You've got to stop doing this."

"I know, I know. No investigating, no stopping bad guys." I stopped talking when I saw Deegan shaking his head. His continued stare made me start self-consciously poking strands of my long hair back into my messy bun, or behind my ears. I must look, well, like a woman who'd recently been held hostage and scared out of her mind.

He stepped closer. "That isn't what I'm talking about."

"No?" My breath hitched. I couldn't imagine what else I'd done to disappoint or upset him.

"No." He stepped even closer, shoes practically touching my own. "You've got to stop trying to give me a heart attack."

And before I could blink, his lips touched mine. It was the briefest, softest feather of a kiss. Gone before I was certain it had happened. I blinked up at Deegan. He stared down at me.

And then Jinx yowled, severing the moment.

"Don't tell me after I came and rescued you, that suddenly this beast of yours doesn't like me?"

"He doesn't like to share." A glance at my watch and the late hour surprised me. "Plus, he's probably hungry. We better find Margo and do whatever statement giving you need so we can get out of here."

"If I told you to stay here, you'd just wander off on your own?" he asked with a frown.

"Yep."

"Fine." Deegan eyed Jinx, then glanced back at me. "I plan to finish our previous conversation, however. Over dinner, at a nice five-star restaurant where they don't allow animals, especially cats, tomorrow night."

And just like that, I had a date for Valentine's Day.

Nine

By the time I recovered my voice after Deegan's surprising declaration of dinner plans, we were going in the wrong direction.

"Margo's aunt's room is actually down this way, I think." Turning, I assumed Deegan would follow. Margo was exactly the distraction I needed right now.

What I didn't plan on was Margo being able to read my face so well.

"Well, hot-diggity-dog!" She slapped the bed beside Mildred as we walked in. "You two finally pulled your heads out and realized you're perfect for each other."

I spluttered.

Deegan cleared his throat.

Jinx spotted a window of escape and jumped down, rushing to the bed. Mildred smiled, petting him as if they were long-lost friends.

"We found Lola," I blurted.

Thankfully, Margo was content with my redirecting of the conversation. At least for now.

"Wonderful!" She craned her neck to look behind me. "Where is she?"

"She is playing nurse to nurse Benjamin. He got another crack over the head after we left you."

"Poor guy." She pointed up. "The lights all came back on. Does that mean everything is fine again?"

Deegan's phone rang. After a short conversation, he nodded and hung up. "Actually, yes." He answered Margo and then explained to all of us that Mr. Leach had just been apprehended trying to flee down the elevator. Unfortunately for him, they were still down for maintenance even though the rest of the power was restored.

The use of his cell phone reminded me of something. "Our phones stopped working shortly after you and I spoke earlier this afternoon." I pulled mine from my pocket. All the bars were back. "They're working now though. Surely that can't be explained by the computer virus, can it?"

"Nope. Turns out, they had a separate phone jammer to block frequencies." Deegan received another call. This one was much shorter. When he hung up, he said, "We're all clear to exit. Leach and Zuri were the only two involved in today's events. Leach admitted, happily apparently, to being the tech genius who installed the virus and set up the signal jammer. Monday is soon enough for statements since we basically have all we need, or expect to get the rest of the confessions from them once Leach and Zuri are behind bars."

The picture in my head of Leach contentedly smiling his serene smile as he confessed gave me the creeps. Pushing the image far, far away, I walked to the bed and gave Mildred a hug. "Thanks for your help today. I hope your recovery is quick and you can go home soon," I said as I picked up Jinx. Mildred's bed was covered in white cat fur, but she didn't seem to mind. She scratched my friendly feline under the chin and bid us both a good evening.

"Can I walk you ladies to your car?"

Margo waved her hand at Deegan's offer. "Thanks, but I'll pass. I'm going to hang out with Aunt Mildred a bit longer." She pulled out her own phone. "I better tell Rita that we're okay though. She might drive up here and murder me herself, otherwise."

"Bye." I waved.

We made our way to the stairwell.

"So, about tomorrow." I quirked an eyebrow.

"Detective Sota!" A squawking voice yelled from the stair entrance. "Can I get your help with something?"

He sighed. With a quick squeeze of my hand, he leaned in and whispered, "I'll pick you up at seven."

As I watched him stride to the stairs and follow the man in uniform down, I pressed my back to the wall and considered how lucky I was. I survived no small amount of crazy today, was rescued by the world's crankiest cat and dishiest detective, and came out not only unscathed but excited about tomorrow's date.

Plus, with that one little kiss my headache had vanished completely.

My stomach, on the other hand, was in knots.

What the heck was I going to wear?

Bonus Epilogue

"You weren't kidding about a five-star restaurant!" I stared in awe at the dazzling chandelier, the white table-cloth covered tables, and the black-tie dressed servers.

Any other inane comments I had were thankfully cut off as we were led to a table in a niche beside a fountain.

An actual fountain. In a restaurant. Clearly, I'd been eating at all the wrong places. Accepting a menu, I noted the obvious lack of prices next to the elaborate appetizers and entrées. Probably a good sign of why I'd never eaten here before; I liked to know what my food cost before I scarfed it down.

"How did you find this place?" I asked.

Deegan looked up from the menu, giving a shrug. "Chief has been talking about it for ages. It seemed like the right place for tonight."

"Did he also happen to say what was good here?"

"Everything. Rumor has it, the dessert menu is longer than the dinner menu."

I pretended to slap at him with the menu. "That doesn't exactly make my choice any easier." It was the truth. *Whisk Me Away* boasted food from countries across the world. Their theme of whisking your palette off to new and exciting destinations meant that escargot, Cajun fondue, and nachos grande all shared space on the same menu. And those were only appetizers!

I settled on blackened chicken smothered with crawfish fondue and a side of garlic mashed potatoes. Mostly because I was afraid what the steak prices might actually be. This was a first date, after all, might as well not scare the man out of a second one. Plus, there was dessert to consider.

"I'll have the prime rib, steak fries, and bacon green beans." Deegan handed our menus to the server after ordering.

"So." *Good job.* I mentally rebuked myself for my conversational eloquence.

"So." Deegan said.

And I couldn't help it. I snorted with laughter.

"Don't tell me we have nothing to talk about if there is no body, no crime, no mystery?"

"I don't think that's the case at all." Deegan tilted his head. "We can talk about the weather."

"Or the number of people in the restaurant." I glanced around as if to count them.

"The proximity of both a fountain and a palm tree to what appears to be a small pyramid and a river." He raised a finger to point behind me. Sure enough, a miniature little Egypt was in the next room.

"That last one is definitely on my top three list," I joked. "What about you?"

"I do have one question that I've been dying to know the answer to."

My curiosity piqued. "And what would that be, exactly?"

He leaned forward. "Why do you always say you have light, light, light, light brown hair? Why not blonde?"

It was not what I'd expected. At the same time, I was surprised he'd never asked before. "It is light, light, light, light brown. It is," I insisted when he shot a raised eyebrow glance of disbelief my way. "It darkens up when it is wet. That's the color it really is. And I don't like to be called blonde because when I was in school, I was very shy and it caused me to have a slight lisp. I got made fun of for being a 'dumb blonde' for years because reading out loud was difficult for me. So, I prefer people know right away that my hair isn't blonde."

"Fair enough."

I unclenched my fingers from the napkin that I hadn't realized I was strangling beneath the table.

"But," he said, "nobody who's met you could possibly think you're dumb, regardless of hair color. You are smart, sassy, and kind, albeit a tad impulsive."

"Just a tad?"

"No, but I thought I was probably better off sticking with saying nicer things on our first date."

"You're lucky we don't have food yet or I'd throw some at you."

"See. My point exactly." Deegan lifted his palms as if to say he rested his case. "It's also apparently dangerous to celebrate the holidays near you."

"Well, at least we're done with holidays for a while. I'm sure everything was just a fluke and life will be going back to normal."

"For once, you and I agree."

"Really?" I tried to snap my jaw shut as shock dropped it open.

"Yep. After all, the next holiday is St. Patrick's Day." Deegan smiled.

I tilted my head. "What does that have to do with anything?"

Steepling his fingers together, Deegan grinned. "March is one of the lowest months for crime, statistically speaking. Especially homicide."

There was a twinkle in his eye and I didn't know if that was good or bad. "Is that true?" I couldn't help but ask.

"I looked it up." Deegan nodded, then frowned. "Though maybe you should plant a lot of four-leaf clovers, just to be sure. You know, for good luck."

The End

Biography

Katherine Brown is a Texas girl, weaver of words, book lover, wife and mom. She put together her first books with paper, cardboard, wrapping paper and ribbon as a child. Her love of books and words stayed with her and as an adult she latched on to the dream of writing full time after years of working in an office job that made her wish for a window in her cubicle to jump out of. Filled with wit and sarcasm plus strong characters that draw you in, Katherine prides herself on writing fun but clean fiction for readers of any age.

https://mailchi.mp/812159f36776/cozy-anthology-back-matter-landing-page

Please consider leaving an online review if you enjoyed reading this book.

Other Fiction Books by Katherine Brown

Sassy Supplies Cozy Mystery Series:

Costumes & Cadavers

Turkeys & Tragedy

Gingerbread & Gravediggers

Hearts & Hostages

Pinches & Peril

Bunnies & Burglaries

Ooey Gooey Bakery Mystery Series:

Rest, Relax, Run for Your Life

Pastries, Pies, & Poison

Bake, Eat, & Be Buried

Savory, Sweet, & Scandalous

Couches & Catastrophes (Book 3.5)

Red Velvet & Romance (Book 4.5) A Valentine's Short

White Chocolate, Weapons, & a Walk Down the Aisle (Book 5)

Young Adult/Fantasy Romantic Mystery & Adventure

The Librarian's Treasure

Children's Books

Princess Bethani's First Garden Party

Princess Bethani's Surprise Visitor

Ghost Boy Camps Out

Tiny Princess & the Big Llama Drama

Becky Beats the Mean Girls

Adventures of Gladys (Ooey Gooey Spinoff Series)

Bonbon Voyage

Half-Baked Homecoming

Non-Fiction / Gift Books by Katherine Brown

Books for Mom

Being a BONUS Mom is…

Being a Mom is… (A little Book of Big Laughs)

Books for Teens & Women

Just a Girl, Dreaming of a Wedding (A Faith-Filled Wedding Planning Journal) available in four styles below:

Pineapple Cover

Red Roses Cover

White Lace Cover

Rose Gold Glitter Cover